D0497988

The Relation of
My Imprisonment

for Sandy —
his copy.
Something to rattle
your cage.
Love,
Russell

Other Books by Russell Banks

The Relation of My Imprisonment

A Fiction by
Russell Banks

Sun & Moon Press
Washington D.C. and *Philadelphia*

This novel was published previously in *United Artists* magazine.

chapter headings by Colleen McCallion

Library of Congress Cataloging in Publication Data

Banks, Russell, 1940-
  The relation of my imprisonment.

  (Contemporary literature series; no. 19)
  I. Title. II. Series: Contemporary literature
series (Sun & Moon Press); no. 19
PS3552.A49R4 1983   813'.54   83-17873
ISBN 0-940650-25-8
ISBN 0-940650-24-X (lim. signed ed.)

FIRST EDITION

1 2 3 4 5 6 7 8 9

Sun & Moon Press
4330 Hartwick Road
College Park, Maryland 20740

For F. Q. H.

''Remember death.''

PON the dawn this drear and soppy month just past, in a year now some twelve years past, it happened that as I began my daily work at the building of coffins, which is my calling, I was prevailed upon by certain superior officers of the town to cease and desist from this work. I had left my young wife's kitchen and had arrived at my workshop at the side of the house and before the road, where, as had been my procedure since completing the apprenticeship of my youth and embarking singly upon the practice of this my calling, I had commenced to lay out the day's labor and to organize that labor into precise allotments of time. Thus I was bent over my various plans and figures at my bench, when there appeared at the doorway a friend and neighbor, a man who must be nameless here but who was one of my chief supports in the early days of my tribulation. This man, all breathless and screw-faced with haste and concern, related to me that this very morning, while passing through the marketplace across the common from the courthouse, as he was on his way to cultivate his fields, which lay on the far side of the town from his dwelling place, he had learned that the chief of civil prosecution in the parish had sent an order to the chief of civil prosecution in the town, to the effect that from this date forward all those men and women residents of this town who engage in the manufacture and/or sale of coffins, or of gravestones or of other such markers of graves, or of vestments for the dead, or of floral or other memorializings of the dead, or who in any way embalm, decorate or otherwise handle and prepare the dead for burial, must henceforth cease and desist from their activities. If this order is not immediately obeyed by those residents of this town who heretofore have participated in such activities, they will be arrested and charged with the crime of heresy and prosecuted to the fullest extent of the various laws.

Because my friend loved me, he wished, however, to do more than merely to warn me of my impending arrest and trial and imprisonment. He attempted as well to persuade me to close the doors of my shop immediately and, upon the eventual arrival at my shop by the officers of the chief of civil prosecution in the town, to deny that I was engaged now in any such activity as had become so recently a heretical activity, for, as my friend pointed out to me, I was an esteemed member of the community, welcomed among them for my comportment and orderliness and the consistent charity of my mind, and therefore the officers of the community would be reluctant to scourge me from them. My skills as a maker of coffins, my friend showed me, could easily be applied to the manufacture of items which the community felt it needed, rather than items which it had deemed not only unnecessary but dangerous to the public weal. He then told me of a growing desire among the better-off families for high wooden cabinets with glass doors for the purpose of exhibiting fragile and expensive possessions.

Having delivered himself both of his warning, which I

received with gratitude, and his suggestion regarding my future activities, which I received with the thought that my friend was perhaps putting his timorous self in my place (out of his love and fear for me, however, not of love or fear for himself), he began to gather up my drawings and figures and contracts for the several coffins I then had underway, wrinkling and folding them as if to toss them into the fire.

No, I said to him. This seems not to be our only recourse. Let us think a moment and look into our hearts before we decide what is the proper action. How would it seem to others of our persuasion, with regard to the matter of the dead, if their coffin-maker were to run and hide and, if found, lie outright? Come, I said to him, be of good cheer, let us not be so easily daunted, our case, to care for the dead, is good, so good that we will be well rewarded, finally, if we suffer for that cause. If, however, we deny our cause, and others like us, seeing our example, also deny the cause, then we will suffer ten hundred and infinitely more times over for the denial. For if we will not remember the dead, who among the living will remember us when we join the dead ourselves, as all men must? (I Craig., xiv, 12.)

My friend persisted and pleaded with me none the less, until I begged leave finally to closet myself briefly for prayer and guidance in this question and proceeded to close myself into the coffin that my father had employed his brother, the revered master to my apprenticeship many years ago, to build for me. And as so often has occurred in times of woe or quandary, the face of a beloved ancestor, in this case the wise face of my mother's great aunt, passed before me and gave me these words: Your guide in life can proceed from no other source than the mercy you tender the dead. To suffer for such tenderness is to receive mercy back from the dead when no others will show it to you.

Whereupon I arose from my coffin and confronted my good friend with these words: Leave me, if you wish, and tend your fields, and turn your coffin into a sideboard, if fear is what determines your actions. But as your fellow man who loves you, I am compelled to go on as before. I further stated that since coming to know myself, I had showed myself hearty and courageous in my coffin-making and had made it my business to encourage and teach others the skills and the meanings of the skills I now possessed, and therefore, thought I, if I should now run and make an escape, it would be of a very ill savour in the land. For what would my weak and newly converted brethren think of it? Nothing but that I was not so strong in deed as I had been privately in word. Also I feared that if I should run now when there may well be a warrant out for my arrest, I might by so doing make them afraid to stand forth some time after when but great words only should be spoken to them. And still further, I thought the world thereby would take occasion at my cowardliness, to have thus blasphemed the dead, to have then some ground amongst themselves to suspect the worst of me and my profession.

Sadly, but with freshened understanding, my friend clasped me to his bosom and departed for his fields, and I retrieved my wrinkled and folded drawings and figures and continued as before to lay out the day's work. And at a quarter past ten in the morning, while I was planing a mahogany headboard for the coffin of a young woman living in a village seven miles from ours, three officers of the chief of civil prosecution in our town entered my shop and read to me the orders issued by the chief of civil prosecution in the parish and by that perogative ordered me to cease and desist my activities as a maker of coffins. I carefully restated all the arguments above, and I continued with my planing as before. The officer in charge, a decent man I have known since we were schoolmates together, then placed me under arrest, and after having released me into my own custody on my own recognizance, wrote out a summons, that I was to appear the following morning at the court of the chief of civil prosecution in the town, there to be heard for indictment and if indicted to be remanded to the parish jail to stand trial at some future date for the crime of heresy. He escorted me outside my shop to where my wife anxiously awaited me and closed and sealed the door to my shop and posted the summons thereon. He was a peaceable and methodical man, as were the junior officers with him, and I believe that they persecuted me only with grave reluctance. May they be remembered, therefore, at least for their inclinations to mercy, even if it happened that they were too weak to enact said mercy. (*II Vis.*, xxx, 4.)

Upon the following day, at a quarter of nine in the morning, I presented myself, in the company of my good wife, who had fearfully dispatched our five children to the home of her cousin in an adjacent parish, at the court of the chief of civil prosecution in our town. Here follows the sum of my examination by His Honor Mister Dome.

Dome: What is the work that you practice in the wooden structure attached to your dwelling place and facing the roadway? And how long have you been at that work?

Self: I am a builder of coffins for the express purpose of tendering mercy to the dead. And I have been such since boyhood, when it became imperfectly known to me that any skills I might obtain while among the living would be without meaning unless bent wholly to that purpose.

Dome: You admit, thereby, that you have all your adult life participated in an activity that the larger community has now declared illegal. Do you also admit that you have consistently and diligently enjoined others to do likewise?

Self: Only those others who give evidence of possessing such gifts as I possess and who, with long instruction and example, can acquire the necessary skills for coffin-building. To those who give no evidence of possessing these gifts, and who therefore ought not to be encouraged to acquire these skills, I merely encourage in a general way to know themselves, so that they may pursue a more truly characteristic way of tendering mercy to the dead. For while there are many paths homeward, there is but a single calling. (*Trib.*, vii, 38.)

Dome: Do you admit that you meet together privately for the purposes of giving and receiving instruction?

Self: It has always been customary to do so in this land, and more efficient also.

Dome: You have before me this day confessed to acts which, though in the past have merely been heinous in the eyes of the community, are henceforth regarded as illegal and, therefore, punishable by law. As is my sworn duty, then, unless you first swear before me at this table that all such activities will no longer be tolerated by you or by those under your care, I will be compelled to indict you for persisting in heresy and to remand you to stand trial in the court of the chief of civil prosecution in the parish. Do you so swear?

Self: I cannot of my own will free the dead from the care of the living, any more than I can of my own will free the living from the care of the dead. It is in the nature of things.

At which words His Honor Mister Dome was in a chafe, as it appeared, for he declared that he would snap the neck of these heresies.

Self: It may be so. But I am not able to aid you, for I am already bound over.

Dome: I find against you, Sir. But if you can locate sureties to be now set for you and thus guarantee that you will appear as ordered for trial at the next quarter-sessions, and also that you will cease and desist, pending the findings of said trial, all coffin-making and other such activities as have been declared illegal, I will set you over to return to your home and family until you are called to court.

Self: I understand that any sureties I obtain will be bound against my further coffin-making, and that if I do build a coffin, their bounds will be forfeited. But since I will not leave off the building of coffins, for I believe this is a work that has no hurt in it but is rather more worthy of commendation than blame, then any who will provide sureties for me will soon hate me. I do not believe that I will be able to uncover any friends willing to provide sureties for me who would also be willing to hate me.

Whereat he told me that if my friends would not be so bound, my mittimus must be made and I sent to the jail and there to lie to the quarter-sessions, some nine weeks off.

Thus have I in short declared the manner and occasion of my first being in prison, where I lie even now, calm in the knowledge that to suffer as a result of the errors and weakness of the living is to be all the more prepared for the demands made by the dead. Let the rage and malice of the living be never so great, they can go no further than the dead will permit them. Even when they have done their worst, I will yet love only that greater power over them, the everlasting dead.

AT the very commencement of my imprisonment it was one of the chiefest pleasures of my days to converse at intermittent times in his rounds with my jailor, whose father had been a higgler from my own town and who often had spoken fondly of my own father to this said man when he was himself a child. It was his recognition of my surname, therefore, that brought him to present himself to me early on my first morning in confinement there. Thus my jailor seemed from the outset to rest in a certain sympathy toward me, for he could not understand how I was a dangerous man that had to be locked away from the company of my fellows, like some beast whose uncontrollable lust it was to tear at living flesh. Nor could it be shown to him that I had destroyed or stolen private or public property or that I had made any claims or abridgements against the lawful liberties of other men.

Yet despite this wondering of why it was that I had been imprisoned, my jailor all the same could not understand why I did not leave off my activities as a maker of coffins and apply my skills instead to some task that the majority of my fellow men wished to see promoted, such as the building of glass-fronted cabinets (he cited the same fashion among the newly wealthy as had my friend earlier, prior to my arrest).

But I have met my calling and the meaning it lends to

my formlessness more sweetly here in this cell than in the world outside, I told him. To show it my back and numbly acquiesce to the demands of the majority of the living would sour the very air that fills my body.

Could you not do more good if you were set at liberty than you can while locked here in a cage? my jailor inquired. He was a decent fellow, and I did believe and believe especially now, many years after his passing away from me, that he was concerned that the most good be done. And what in particular offended him about my confinement was that it seemed to do no one any good. He was thus a man whose compassion was essentially an act of logic, and his view of mean and cruel men was that they were merely illogical. We could not agree on this, for my own view has been that such men are mean and cruel because they will not perform the rites and other acts of worship which would purge them of their meanness and cruelty, which purgation would thereby permit them to enact goodness in the world. Mercy, I explained to my jailor, is a quality of feeling toward others that must be obtained at some source outside the human heart. My brethren and I believe that it can only be obtained by devoting oneself fully to the worship and further contemplation of the power of the dead. For a man cannot see or hear or touch the world born and dying daily around him until he has first seen, heard and touched the infinite. (*Wal.*, v, 41.)

When I had lain in prison for along about twelve weeks, and not during that time knowing what they intended to do with me, upon the fifteenth of May there came to me a Mister Jones, clerk of the court, having been sent by the

several justices of the parish to admonish me and demand
of me submission to their regulation of my activities and
the curtailment of any future making of coffins or of teaching others to do likewise or of recommending such activities and the wisdom and sweetness thereof to any others,
especially to the youth. But since I knew that my case had
not yet been publicly tried and that I was merely under
indictment and had not yet confessed to any act of heresy
but had merely argued as to the legitimacy and rightness
of my calling, I knew the admonitions and demands put
to me by Mister Jones were but part of a strategem designed
to control me without having as well to defend in public
the court's interest in breaking the neck of the people's
growing love for the dead and their gradual awakening to
acts of worship and contemplation of the dead. For, as all
men knew, there was in those years a new spirit moving
over the land which was compelling the people toward a
deeper delight in life that was by necessity and grace de-
rived from their growing knowledge and experience of the
dead. The finite is but the flesh of the infinite, and the living the breath of the dead. (*Flor.*, ii, 14.) Here is how
Mister Jones, clerk of the court, made his conversation
with me:

When he was come into my chamber, which I had in
various ways and through the aid of my young wife made
as comfortable and cheerful as such a stony place could be
made, he called heartily out to me, Neighbor! How do you
do, neighbor?

I thank you, Sir, said I. Very well, blessed be the dead.

Said he, scratching at his nose, Well, Sir, I have come to
tell you that it is desired that you would submit yourself

unto the laws of the land, or else at the next quarter-sessions it will go far worse with you, even to be banished and sent away from out of the nation or else even worse than that.

I said with all seriousness, looking briefly onto the face of my jailor for confirmation, that I did desire only to demean myself in the world, as becometh a man and a worshipper of the dead. Whatever denied me that benefit could not be pursued, I explained.

Still he scratched his nose, as if there were situated there some devious growth or some question that by a steady scratching would get answered. You must leave off these unholy and illegal practices which you have long been wont to participate in and endorse among others, for the statute is now set up against them, and here am I now, sent by the justices to tell you that they do intend to prosecute the law against you if you will not submit.

Sir, I said modestly but with natural authority and a reasonable man's knowledge of procedure and law, Sir, I conceive that the laws by which I am imprisoned at this time, the laws of indictment, do not reach or condemn either me or the practices of tendering mercy in various accepted, codified manners to the dead. I have come forward and made myself known unto the world, and now you and your justices must do the same. The dead will decide who is in the right.

I believe that the clerk of the court was a weak and easily frightened man, for at this he turned and stalked furiously from my presence. My jailor was at first moved to laughter, but after a moment, when he saw that mirth had not been my intent, he sombered and declared his affection for my methods, though he said he was repelled by my cause. This did not dismay or discourage me, for I had long ago undergone the type of self-scrutiny that weds method to cause, and therefore I knew my jailor's lack of affection for my cause was only due to his ignorance of it, whereas his appreciation of what he called my methods could only be due to a clear readiness for conversion.

And indeed, before the next quarter-sessions came to term, my jailor, whose name was John Bethel, had begun to open his heart and understanding to the mystery of the dead and had commenced joining me in my cell for evening prayer and contemplation. He had not yet his own coffin and therefore was compelled to close himself in his arms where two walls meet, as is the custom for those among the brethren who, for reasons, have not their own coffins at ready access. But when he had frequently observed my emergence from prayer and had glimpsed indirectly thereby the grace and relief obtained, he thereupon had each time attempted to elicit from me the name of one by whom he himself might have a coffin built.

I greeted his repeated request with deeply troubled feelings. On the one hand, I took delight from what appeared to be a case of genuine conversion to the understanding that supercedes all understanding, and I knew that without his own coffin in which to closet himself for prayer and contemplation, my brother John Bethel would eventually see his questing fall back upon itself, like a vine with nothing to attach itself to, there to wither and die. This possibility, nay, this likelihood! grieved me, and I would determine at once to provide him with the name of one of those among us who would build him a coffin,

when, as I paced my cell waiting for my jailor to make
his evening round and appear to me, it would seem to me
that his request for information, such as the name of one
who would build him a coffin, was but a subtle ruse designed to induce me to expose and incriminate and thereby condemn one of my beloved brethren to the fate I now
endured. And thus I would close my mind as if it were a
fist, and I would swear never to reveal the names of my
fellow worshippers of the dead, even if tortured and
brought to the very gateway of death itself. I had no fear
of torture in those years, any more than I do today, for I
was filled with the knowledge that if one among the living
were to bring me to the very gateway of death and there
threaten to hurl me through, it would be as if he were
threatening to hurl me into the arms of my dead parents
and long-departed ancestors, and I would at such a
moment urge him onward, not to confound him, as I am
sure it would do, but so as to end this agony of separation.

While I was yet enduring this quandary with regard to
the question of the conversion of my jailor John Bethel,
as it was now some weeks beyond the second quarter-
sessions of the meeting of the justices of the parish for the
purposes of trying all those previously indicted and not yet
tried in public court and still I had not yet been called
forth so to be tried, though I continued to languish in jail
fully as if I had indeed been tried and convicted of those
crimes for which I had merely been indicted and had not
confessed (except as to argue against the legitimacy of the
laws which prohibit acts of worship of the dead such as
my brethren are known to participate in), came the time of
the solstice. Now at the solstice there is usually a general

releasement of divers prisoners, by virtue since ancient days of the high feelings surrounding the event, in which privilege I also should have had my share. But they would not take me for a convicted person, unless I were willing to sue out a pardon (as they called it), by means of which I would recant all my previous statements and activities as had got me indicted in the first place. Therefore, since I was no more willing under these new circumstances to recant and deny than I had been when under more durable and oppressing circumstances twenty weeks before, I could have no benefit of the solstice. Whereupon, while I continued in prison, my good wife went unto the several justices, that I might be heard and that they would impartially take my case into public consideration.

There were three, and the first that my wife did plead unto was Judge Hale, who was celebrated for his learning and deep probity and who was known for his leniency towards dissenters of various sorts. He very mildly received her, telling her that he would do her and me the best good he could, but he feared, said he, that he could do none.

The following day, lest the judges should, by the multitude of their business, forget me, she did throw another petition onto the table of Judge Twisdom, who, when he saw it and had read it through, snapped her up and angrily informed her that I was a convicted person already and could not be released unless I would promise to make no more coffins and not to teach others, &c.

After this disappointment, she went unto Judge Bester, who, in the mild presence of Judge Hale, stood and declared loudly and angrily that I was convicted by the court and that I was a hot spirited fellow, whereat he waved the petition in the air above his head and shouted that he would not meddle therewith.

But yet my wife, being encouraged by the seeming kindly face and manner of Judge Hale, did persist, saying that I had been indicted merely and had confessed to no crime and had not been tried, yet I was both confined to prison and at the same time was not to receive the indulgences prompted by the solstice that all other prisoners were to be granted. The place where this interview took place was called the Lion's Chamber, where there were then situated the two judges and also many gentry and officers of the several towns in the parish. My wife, coming into them with a bashed face and a trembling heart and voice, began her errand to them in this manner:

Woman: My Lord (directing herself to Judge Hale), I make bold to come once again to your Lordship to know what may be done with my husband.

Hale: Woman, I have told you that I can do you and your husband no good, because they have taken that for a conviction which your husband has already spoken at the indictment. And unless there be something done to un-do that, I can do you no good.

Woman: My Lord, he was clapped into prison . . .

One of the gentry in the room, interrupting her: My Lord, the man was lawfully convicted! Why waste your precious time?

Woman: False! False!

Whereupon Judge Bester answered very angrily, saying that my wife must think that judges could do whatever they wished, whereas it seemed instead that her husband, meaning me, was the one who at this very moment was standing at prison for attempting to do whatever he wished. Did she desire that they too, meaning the judges and various gentry in the room, should end standing in prison alongside her husband? He laughed loudly at this.

Woman: But my Lord, he was not lawfully convicted.

Bester: He was.

Woman: No, he was not.

Bester: Indeed he was!

Hale: He was.

One of the gentry: Get this woman from out the room! She is a disrupter!

Bester: He was convicted! It is recorded! It is recorded! he continued crying, as if it must be of necessity true because it was so recorded. With which words, he and the others in the chamber, for they had taken up the cry, attempted to stop up her mouth, having no other argument to convince her but, It is recorded! It is recorded!

Here Judge Hale, trying to restore order, but not so greatly interested in restoring justice, interrupted and declared that none should talk about this matter any further, for he (meaning me) cannot do whatever he wishes, and he (meaning me again) has proved himself a breaker of the peace if not a heretic.

Woman: He only desired to live peaceably and that he follow his calling, both that his life and his family's be properly maintained, and moreover, my Lord, I have five small children that cannot help themselves, of which one is born blind, and they and I now have nothing to live upon but the charity of good people.

Hale: You have five children? You are but a young

woman to have five children. And a slender woman to have five children. (He seemed to wish her proven a liar of some sort.)

Woman: I am, my Lord, but stepmother to them, having not been married to him yet two full years when he was first arrested. Indeed, I was with child when my husband was first apprehended, but being young and unaccustomed to such things then, I was smayed at the news and fell into labor and so continued for eight days, then was delivered, but my child died.

Whereat Judge Hale, looking very soberly on the matter, said, Alas, poor woman!

But Judge Bester declared that she made poverty and pain her cloak and its lining.

Here the woman fell to weeping, albeit in silence, for while she had up to now endured great woe and tribulation, this attack upon her very integrity, coming as it did from such a height and, as it seemed to her then and to me now, with no other cause than that of idle malice, came with a heaviness all out of proportion to its mass, as if it were a chain cast from lead and placed around her narrow shoulders solely to bear her down.

When she had left this place called the Lion's Chamber and had brought herself directly to my cell and had recounted to me the details of her several interviews with these mighty persons, I saw that it would be this way with me now for my life time, unless I could contrive to get my name placed upon the calendar for the quarter-sessions of the meeting of the court and thus could come to trial and either be found innocent, and freed in that way, or else be convicted, and thence freed by the power of the general amnesty associated with the solstice. While my wife wept in despair, for she had at last given up the fight for my freedom, I negotiated with my jailor, who, at my direction, had determined to obtain the calendar for the quarter-sessions of the meeting of the court and place my name thereon, thus compelling the justices to hear my case, for, with my name upon that calendar, they would have no choice but to call me to come forward. I allowed myself the pleasure of admiring the symmetry between their claim that my confession and judgement were already recorded and my own new claim that my name was recorded upon the calendar. Their foolish worship of the record would compel them to proceed in a manner that they had earlier deemed undesirable if not wholly repellent.

My jailor, John Bethel, here proved his devotion to my cause, as well as to my method, for he went out from me and under the cover of darkness stole into the courthouse where the records were kept and added my name to the calendar, so that the following day, when he was instructed by an officer of the court to deliver the various named prisoners who were to be tried that day, he was able to come to my cell and bring me forth. As I passed him in the hallway, I whispered unto him that he would soon have the coffin he required, and together, I and seven other prisoners, under the careful guard of my brother John Bethel and his two assistants, came to the courthouse, there to present ourselves for trial.

I was not at first noticed standing among the others in the docket, but before long one of the justices, Judge Bester, saw me there and signalled in whispers to the other two judges that I was present, whereupon all three began to glare heatedly at me while they listened to the various cases being put before them. This glaring of theirs distracted them somewhat, for on several occasions they compelled the prisoner before them to repeat his testimony of defense, and in all seven cases they were able to agree unanimously on the guilt of the prisoner before them, even without the usual discussion amongst themselves, so as to hurry toward the calling out of my name. This calling duly came, whereupon Judge Bester reddened with fury and with a roar charged that I had somehow contrived to alter the calendar and that he would see me punished horribly for such a crime. Judge Hale, more calmly than his brother judge but in a rage none the less, called my jailor forth and put to him these questions:

Hale: John Bethel, you were posted throughout the night in your office at the prison, were you not?

Jailor: It is my duty, Sir.

Hale: Did this man pass you or was he in any way absent from his cell during the night?

Jailor: No, Sir, he did not and he was not.

Hale: How, then, do you think he altered the calendar?

Jailor: I am but a jailor, Sir, and thus I have no thoughts on the matter. Since, however, it was recorded that he was to be brought to trial here today, I did not know what else to do with him but to bring him straightway here so that you might try him. To delay or otherwise obstruct his being tried, Sir, would be to foul the law and the numerous statutes of procedure.

Bester (interrupting): The calendar has been secretly altered! Hang him for it! We shall try him, oh, we shall try him indeed, but we shall try him for altering the calendar! (He was at this point too vexed to continue speaking and began to sound as if he were chewing upon a piece of cloth, and he left off trying to speak and instead turned away and faced the back of the courtroom in a fume.)

Hale: Have you (meaning me) anything to say for your defense?

Self: With what, Sir, am I charged?

Hale: With having altered the calendar.

Self: I have not been properly indicted for that crime, Sir. I have been indicted only for the crime of heresy, to which I have not confessed, and therefore I do not believe I can be tried for the crime of altering the calendar.

This threw the three justices into a deep uproar, and the numerous observers and gentry attending the scene broke into loud laughter and guffaws. For it was now clear to all that the justices had tangled themselves in the cords and folds of their own procedure and that all their combined anger could not disentangle them. It was also clear that they would, in spite of themselves, try me this day, for one crime if not for another, and probably for no better reason than that they were being driven to it by their anger.

Hale: If your name is on the calendar, then we shall indeed try you, Sir! And the crime for which we shall try you is that of having altered the court calendar! As for the crime of heresy, for which you have already been duly indicted and to which you have confessed, it is recorded that you were, by virtue of your recorded confession, condemned in absentia, that is to say, without public trial, and thus you shall still remain ineligible for the pardon occasioned by the solstice, which applies only to those duly convicted at a public trial and now standing at prison. This new trial and the conviction that will doubtless follow shall bring with it the death penalty. And from that there shall be no pardon also! You, Sir, and all your followers, shall learn that the procedures of law exist to protect the rights of the law-abiding. They shall not be abused by those who, like yourself, wish to subvert and destroy justice! (Here he fell into a confused and angry tirade against tax evaders and other petty criminals, wandering in his words, it seemed to me, until at last he tailed off among mumbled phrases and uncompleted sentences.)

Then my brother, my jailor, came forward, and by his intelligence and courage and his love for me, made me crack with shame, for he had discerned what, in my pleasure at having discomfited the several justices, I had not discerned. He had seen that if I were to be tried for having altered the calendar, I would be swiftly convicted, for the justices, even the saintly Hale, were in such a temper as to find no one now before them innocent, and he had seen that they were ready to condemn a man to hard labor for life, if given the chance, for no greater crime than that of misspelling the name of the month. My brother had also seen what I had deliberately allowed myself to be blinded to: he had seen that they would hang me for the crime of altering the calendar. And therefore, he had determined, by virtue of his old life's values, that I would be far better off languishing for numberless years in a cold damp prison cell than hanging from yonder gallows tree. This meant that while he had been sufficiently converted to my teachings and example so as to be able to face death courageously himself, he was not sufficiently freed of his old life's courtship of itself to realize that I would be shamed and heartbroken by his taking my place at the gallows.

For these reasons, he came forward to the justices and declared that it had been he, John Bethel, who had altered the calendar so as to include my name upon it, and that if any man were to be tried and convicted for the said crime, it must be he. Let this interview and this assertion stand as an indictment and confession, said John Bethel, and let the clerk of the court properly add my name and blot out the name of the coffinmaker, and let the trial proceed as ordered by the statutes of procedure.

I cried out in vain that he must not sacrifice himself for the living, that he must only sacrifice himself for the dead, as we have long been taught (*II Carol.*, iv, 34-35), but it was too late. Judge Hale ordered the sergeant-at-arms to clap the jailor in irons and to present him in the docket, from which I myself was roughly removed. I saw the jailor's peaceful eyes as I was wrenched past him and he took my place, and I uttered these words: My brother, you shall have my own coffin. Though you are in error, you have earned the right to it, and I have not.

This was the most public event in the twelve years of my imprisonment that have so far transpired, and thus it was the most misunderstood and the most slandered. By this brief private account I have tried to make understanding possible and slander libelous. Also by this account have I tried to tender mercy to the beloved dead man, John Bethel, who in life was my jailor and who in death awaits me as a brother.

MY jailor went forward unto the dead in my stead, and though there sometimes passed through my heart a swift blade of grief, and though I was often, on the occasion of dark and cold afternoons that first autumn of my imprisonment, lashed by regret and shame, I was able to obtain a measure of release from my guilt and comfort for my pain from my having been able to provide him with my own personal coffin for his journey unto the dead, and I was further released and comforted by the sure knowledge that, though he had taken my place among the dead, I was now taking his place among the living. I remembered the old teachings on death, how it must fall to every one of us, and whether it come sooner or later matters not, for time is valueless to the dead. Only the living can be tempted by time; the dead, by their nature, treasure it not at all.

It was during this early period of my imprisonment, when I had not yet obtained a coffin to replace the one I had transferred to my jailor, that I determined to atone for my rashness and stupidity in the matter concerning the alteration of the court calendar. I decided to atone for my life by resisting death. This meant that henceforth I would be compelled to avoid any confrontation that would risk my life. It also meant that I would no longer be able to deny myself any sustenance, any food, rest or medication or other physical comfort that in whatsoever way contributed to the further resistance of death.

I did this, said I to my wife and several friends, all of whom were at first astonished by this change in my behavior, to honor the dead John Bethel and the manner of his dying. My beloved frail wife, who had not yet wholly absorbed the principles and the celestial hugeness of the design that undergirds and guides our faith, was at first inclined to give outward evidence of great pleasure at my determination to avoid all activities and practices that could lead me into a fatal encounter with death. She clasped me to her tender bosom when she first heard of my decision and amid much weeping and wild high laughter exclaimed that now our children would be saved, for, as she saw it, now their father would be saved. And to my surprise and disappointment, she let it out that she now expected me to recant and forswear, as I had been so many times encouraged as well by the justices to do, my life long practice of the making of coffins and the teaching of this skill and the meanings of the skill to others.

No, dear wife, I admonished her. That I will not permit myself to do. For I am now uniquely situated in life, by virtue of my imprisonment, so as to be able to sustain my life and in that way scourge myself for having sinned in the matter of altering the court calendar without, at the same time and by that means, having also to deny the worth and significance of my worship of the dead and my desire to join them. This my life of imprisonment is come to me now as a great opportunity to bless and show mercy to one among them, the man who was my jailor, John Bethel. I cannot, indeed, I must not, let that opportunity slide away. To do so would be to render a meaningful existence meaningless, would be to sow confusion among the brethren, would be to desert my children altogether, and in the end would be to place myself beyond deserving your wifely love, which even now, by my failure to have given you deep enough understanding of my acts, seems to be withdrawing itself from me so as to attach itself back to its source, there to stagnate, a foul perversion of love and not at all the pure spring-like bubbling forth of love that you have carried to me up to now. Sit yourself down here by me in my cell, I said to her, so that I may begin to teach you from the ancient texts the meanings of our movements between life and death, and free me thereby to atone for my prideful oversight and the earlier inadequacy of my teaching, which, even as you exclaim and clasp me to you, reveals itself to us both in the painful form of your thrilled weeping at my new determination not to resist life.

And thereupon did I commence to instruct my young wife from the ancient texts and the myriad examples of death that have come down to us from olden times. And every day she came unto me, often in the company of a relation, to sit for hours and there to listen and reason together and exchange views, until such a time had passed as she did feel that she had fully penetrated my understanding and had taken it unto herself in such a form and thoroughness as to be able to convey it to our children, who, because of the corrupting nature of the prison, were not permitted to visit me during those years. (Later, when the two oldest grew large enough to pass as adults, they were to come unto me, and I will soon describe their visit.)

URING the period of my wife's instruction, there grew within me, in the secret manner of a tumor, a quickly rising desire for fleshly contact with women, that at the start would as quickly, after I had become aware of its presence and had with mild horror rebuked it, weaken and droop back upon itself. This abominable longing would steal upon me and catch me unawares, even as I was deeply immersed in the teachings of the patriarchs and matriarchs or in discussion of theological history with my wife or her cousin (a young woman who sometimes accompanied my wife to the prison), or even when, for we then frequently resorted there, we three would each face a place in the tiny cell where two walls came together and, folding ourselves in our own arms, attempt to pray. These eruptions of lust knew no bounds of decency or decorum, honored no categories of thought, argument or inquiry, nor would they share the stage of my thoughts and sensibilities with any other player. Thus it was only with an enormous effort of will, frequently supplemented by quantities of anger (at my weakness, my own, no demon's strength, no dark deity's), that each time I was able to yank that player off the stage and replace him with the legitimate one.

I cannot deny this depraved interlude, that it existed, that I fought it, to be sure, and that, in the end, I was overcome by it. Nor can I lay the blame at anyone's feet but my own. I confess my transgression against the spirit of the dead, which by its glory and infinitude demands our entire devotional attention. I confess it because I wish to let myself serve as a warning and a lesson to others who may in some future time during a similar period of connubial deprivation find themselves afflicted as was I. Therefore, I beg the reader's indulgence and understanding of the presence, to follow, of certain descriptions that in a less somber, less deliberately instructional work would be reprehensible, if not morally disgusting. And let the prurient minded be warned: there will be nothing of interest for you here, for all that follows is woe and deprivation, and what may appear on the surface to be the glitter of sensual gratification, at bottom is but the enlightening muck and mire of self-disgust.

In those months of her instruction, which was the winter-time of my first year of imprisonment, my wife grew wan and sickly, as a consequence of her sufferings from the birthing of the child born dead the previous spring, and also from the sufferings wrought by the poverty of her life without the presence of a husband able to earn a living in the world. I do also fear that her daily journey to the prison, which was often a damp and chilled place, despite my efforts to warm the cell with the brazier that my new jailor had kindly supplied me, exacerbated her condition somewhat. So that by the middle of December she had gone to a pathetic thinness and her skin had come to be cracked and chafed by the wind and cold, and she was beginning to cough. Even so, each noontime when she arrived at my cell, often bearing freshly baked cakes or bread, she would smile cheerily and fill me with news of our dear children and the lives of our brethren in the faith, most of whom, by having watched me be over-whelmed by the power of the state, had either made their practices of worship invisible to the state or had chosen self-banishment and had gone out of the nation. (This was but one of the reasons why it was then so difficult for me to obtain a new coffin to replace the one I had made over to my saintly jailor, John Bethel.) However, many was the day when, at the arrival of my wife, I peered into her gray eyes and saw the suffering hidden there, and the sight, despite all my efforts against it, often brought me to tears.

After a short time my wife began to see the effect her wretched state was having on me, and so she struggled all the more bravely to disguise it, even to the extreme measure of wearing dresses that exaggerated and pointed with innocent directness to the few remaining curves and rises of her body. She took to wearing a dark blue wool dress that I gathered she had knitted herself during the long evenings alone in our cottage after the children had gone off to bed. This dress, unintentionally provocative, was designed to fit snugly around her hips and buttocks and to lift and round her small breasts so as to make her seem to me more healthy and jocular than in fact she was. I cannot say it forcefully enough, but let it be known to all that my wife in no way was attempting to encourage in me the lust that her presence in that knit dress soon began to provoke. So did I then believe, and so do I be-lieve today. Let this account in no way besmirch her pure and devoted life, her noble death, and the majesty of her present and everlasting existence among the dead. Let it merely serve as a warning to those who, desiring to bring comfort and good cheer to the living, inadvertently wreak havoc and establish depression among them instead. We cannot provide solace for the living, no more than can we avenge ourselves upon the dead. Presence evades attention, absence invites it, and there is no choice, for there is but the acceptance of what is possible, or the denial. (*Trib.*, iv, 13.)

If, then, my dearly beloved wife erred, she erred in this way, and given the brevity of her previous period of instruction in the faith, she was no more to be condemned for her actions than was my jailor John Bethel for his. And to be sure, if anyone is to stand condemned, let me be the one, for I was the only person, in both cases, who could be said to have been responsible for their instruction in the faith, for in both cases did I myself undertake their instruction. Yet I had mistrusted John Bethel's pleas for the name of a coffinmaker, so that he could in life have practiced the uplifting rite of prayer, which would have opened him sufficiently unto the wisdom of the dead so as to have forbidden him from supplanting my death with his own that day in court. The result therefrom must be blamed on me. And I did pridefully assume that my young wife's proximity to me day and night for the two years of our marriage prior to my arrest was sufficient instruction for her to know at once that whatever device she used to provide me with less pity for her, if it awakened in me appetites that drew my attention away from the dead and toward the living, then the device, regardless of her kind intent, was diabolical. No, I am the one who must be

blamed for these two errors in faith. I am the one who has
failed the terms of his calling and who, therefore, must
beg forgiveness of the dead.

It thus happened that one particularly sour and chilled
December noontime, when my wife came unto me and
entered my cell, and when the jailor had left us alone and
had returned to his post below, the close heat of my cell
swiftly brought a blush to her face and encouraged her
to unwrap her scarf and shawl, which revealed in the glow
of the brazier and my reading candle an illusory fullness
through her hips and breasts, an illusory healthy round-
ness to her arms, and great warmth of illusory color in
her throat. I declare it illusory simply because I well knew
that the woman had long been ill and pinched by pain
and that in my absence she had been forced frequently
to deprive herself so that the plates of my children, her
step-children, could be filled. Further, I declare it illusory
so that it may be known abroad that she did in no way
provoke me or otherwise draw from me lustful ambitions.
They existed prior to her arrival that noontime and they
merely used her presence as an occasion to arise and make
themselves known to us. The woman lived purely. She
wished no more than to let me beget a new child upon
her, a child of her own who would be able someday to
tender proper mercy to her when she herself had joined
the blessed dead. I, I was the one who had no pure
thoughts that day, no thoughts of an unborn child coming
to life so as to bless me in death, I was the one whose
lust had no ambition other than its own satisfaction, a
means with no end, a cause with no effect.

Therefore did I reach out and paw her soft body and

draw her to me, and then did I wrench her dress from
her body and expose her creamy surface to the flick of
candle light and the steady glow of the reddened coals in
the brazier, and then did I strip my trousers off, and pulling my wife down, did I cover her with my body and
swarm over her for a great long time, until at last did I
fall away and, exhausted, uncouple from her.

At first, my response to this act was, of all the possible
responses then available to me, the weakest one. I strode
down the path of least resistance, as it were, by simply
refusing to acknowledge this lustful seizure and the sei-
zures that regularly every afternoon followed it, like links
in a binding chain, as being anything more than some
natural expression of my body, no less natural than the
continued growth of the hair of my head or the hair of
my beard or the nails of my fingers and toes. This in-
sistance upon the naturalness of my act was, of course,
as the reader must know all too well, nothing but a means
of construing the situation so as to be better able to repeat
the act, over and over, day after day, until it had become
a hideous habit and there seemed to be no way of separat-
ing the head of it from the tail. Each time after my wife
had wrapped herself once again modestly in her scarf
and shawl and had left my presence, I would groan aloud
and beat my breast with shame, and each time, before
long, I would start up with assurances that what I was
doing was no more than any man's body, so deprived by
imprisonment, would wish him to do. I even contrived a
clever guard against shame by wheedling out of my intelligence this argument: that to berate myself for having
fallen into lustful copulation was to give an unnatural

attention to things and events of this life, which was un-
necessarily and sinfully to pull my proper attention away
from contemplation of the dead. And like a true sophist,
I even used scripture to woo me from self-disgust. Leave
off undue fascination with and morbid examination of
things of the body, I told myself, quoting the sacred book
of *Walter* (x, 42). Thus did I not only debase myself, but
I debased the words of the sainted dead as well. And all
this in but the very beginnings of my period of transgression! I elaborate on and attend to it here solely that
the reader will know that I too have been confronted by
the forces of life that would demean and destroy our faith,
and I too have walked across the barren desert of my own
weakness and have come to the mountains beyond, and I
have at last ascended those mountains. I have endured
as all men may endure, if they will but will it.

From here my debauch, like a tropical river, broadened
and deepened, until it seemed to flow irresistably into a
sea of life, a tepid expanse where nothing but teeming
forgetfulness and transience may exist, where the perman-
ence of remembered death is denied a place and the sin-
gleness of mortal existence, our movement from life to
death, has no meaning. For not only did I begin to curtail
by an increasing amount of time the period of instruction
and prayer each afternoon with my wife, so that I could
squirm and roll with her on the mat in the darkened
corner of my cell, but I began to vary from one day to the
next the modes and positions of our interpenetration.
This was, to be sure, a consequence of the regularity of
our unbridled comings together, a way of avoiding contact
with and recognition of our essential boredom with the

act and our deep knowledge of its superfluity and utter
gratuitousness, for we had long since removed ourselves
from any possible rationalizations such as the begetting of
new children. It may also have been the consequence
of a newly released idle curiosity. (I credit this motive
only to myself; I know that my wife never experienced
such a loathsome provocation.) But whatever the cause,
before long we were engaged in acts that could only be
named beastly, in positions that could only be described
as perverse or, if one were inclined toward compassion,
as pathetic or, if one were maliciously detached, as comic.
And we worked heatedly and furiously, as if we were
about to be interrupted and publicly exposed while in
the midst of our abominations.

Which, unhappily, is what happened. One afternoon in
late December, when my wife and I were feverishly engaged in copulation, from a position that in retrospect
now appears grotesque but which at the time functioned
on my visual sense so as to draw forward from me a great
long surge of erotic attention, my new jailor, a man named
Jacob Moon, suddenly appeared at my cell door, which,
as was the practice with political and religious prisoners,
perpetrators of what were then called crimes of con-
science, lay open and unlocked. It was only at night or
during a rare emergency or during the visit of some legal
dignitary that the cell doors in my section of the prison
were closed and locked. This relative freedom of movement was considered a privilege and, more importantly, a
tacit acknowledgement of the vague and ambiguous terms
of our crimes and the punishments attached thereto, for
during those years both the prisoners and the authorities

felt that it was to their respective group's advantage to
perpetuate for as long as possible the vagueness and
ambiguity of the terms of the crimes and punishments.
Now, of course, both parties have taken the opposite position, which accounts for all the recent bouts of litigation,
the continuous appeals to higher courts, the rising income
of attorneys, and the facts that the cell doors are locked
at all times and that many other amenities, such as my
coal brazier, have been eliminated. For nowadays the
prisoners have come to feel that they must be either
wholly free or wholly imprisoned. In previous years, however, since they had feared that the only alternative available to them was total imprisonment and that total freedom was out of the question, and since the authorities
feared that total freedom was the option and that total
imprisonment was out of the question, both groups had
struggled to achieve the mid-point between, a compromise
that, because it denied both parties' worst fears, satisfied
everyone. At present neither party is satisfied. And therefore, one of my several tasks here, as I see it, is to try to
show both parties the wisdom of the old way.

Jacob Moon was John Bethel's replacement as chief
jailor, but in no other way was he that man's replacement.
He was not unfriendly, and he was not unkind to the
prisoners, neither was he especially efficient nor especially inefficient as manager of our confinement. He had
been, up to this moment of his discovery of my wife and
myself in a particularly humiliating circumstance, a man
who had struck me by his strikingly ordinary manner of
doing his job and by a singular lack of curiosity or interest
in the lives and minds of the often quite interesting and

enriching individuals under his care. He did seem, however, to come to life that afternoon, and with a forth-
rightness that surprised me, he asked if he could join me
and my wife. His request was tenderly put, and because
it came at precisely the moment of my and my wife's
greatest sensual arousal, I signalled him impatiently to
enter the cell and to join us, which he proceeded to do
in quite a matter of fact manner, as if it were his habit
or custom so to find himself on an otherwise uneventful
mid-winter afternoon.

Naturally, I was afterwards filled with great remorse
and shame. Not only had I debauched myself and trans-
gressed the teachings of my faith, but I had also led my
wife, my poor trusting wife, into debauchery and transgression likewise, and here I was now, leading yet a third
person into debauchery and transgression. The fact that
Jacob Moon, or Jake, as we came to call him, was not of
our faith in no way lessened his transgression or my
responsibility for it. The scriptures say, If you would
transport yourself unto the dead, you must also transport
others, and if you refuse to transport others thither, the
gate shall be closed to you also. (*II Craig.*, xxii, 43.)

My wife and Jake attempted to calm me and tried val-
iantly to purge me of guilt by asserting that I was not
responsible for their participation, and for a brief period
I was sufficiently weak and spiritless (in will, for my
appetites were extremely strong) to believe them, so that
I was then of a mind that the only weakness I was con-
tending with, the only one I had to feel guilty for, was
my own, a vain fantasy, I now realize, but one that I
clung to during those horrible months with the desper-

ation of a man drowning in a sea of overpowering desire. During this period I turned with embarrassment away from prayer and scripture, and also I gradually gave up attempting to explain the ethics and metaphysics of my faith, upon which I heretofore had expended great energy, time and ingenuity in conversation with my wife and, now and again when she accompanied my wife, her cousin Gina.

I cannot blame any of these three good people for having joined me in my debauch. I blame only myself, for clearly, if I had not permitted it, if I had not given myself over with such foolish abandon to the physical pleasures offered by my wife's body, if I had not permitted Jake that afternoon to enter my cell but had instead reacted with proper horror and self-loathing at his proposal, and if the following week I had not permitted Gina to give herself over to Jake's demands, and then later had not allowed myself to answer her wild cries for satisfaction or my wife's child-like demands for equal attention from Jake, if at the beginning or at any point along this long, satiny, declining path I had stood up and had said, No! and in that humble way had begun again to turn my attention back to the dead, then none of it would have occurred. I here publicly admit my failure and in this way offer to the dead what meager mercy and remembrance I am capable, in such a fallen state, of offering.

My strength did eventually, though only partially, come back to me, yet it came suddenly, like a room filling with darkness when a candle is extinguished. It came back to me in full force much later, however, and only on the day when I finally obtained my coffin again, an event of great magnitude, coming as it did after such sustained desolation. And then once again would it be proved to me that solely by the careful and proper observation of rite and ceremony and the methodical, informed use of artifact may the mind of the living be permitted the transcendent experience of contemplation of the dead, which in turn is the only way to obtain a proper understanding of the meaning of life. All other means, despite the best of intentions, are but approximate and ultimately misleading. And innocence leads nowhere at all. (*The Book of Discipline*, viii, 23-25.)

How it came to pass that I obtained a new coffin will be described near the end of this testament. In the meantime, let the reader imagine me, in the descriptions to follow immediately, as daily, usually in the afternoons, engaging in the awful practices and depravities I have described above, while during the mornings and evenings I passed my time in peaceful argument with my jailor (for we had become brothers of a sort and an exchange of views between us was a natural extension of our new affiliation) and also with diverse other prisoners who were of a religious turn of mind but who were not of my faith. For my purpose now is to reveal how the mind of the fallen man, the man who has allowed his attention to wander off the dead and fix itself onto the living only, swiftly divides itself into segments, boxes of thought, attitude and activity with no necessary or discernible link, consistency or communication between them, resulting inevitably in that pathetic and sorrowful figure, the man of time.

THE man of time is without self-unity. I was now such a man. Every day early in the day, I hailed my jailor Jacob Moon in his office at the bottom of the stone staircase that spined the prison, and upon first catching sight of his grim and wholly pragmatic face, the face of a man who had long ago made of himself a tool to fit what he regarded as the job of life, I instantly arranged my own face into a matching mask, and because he never signalled with a wave or other such greeting gesture, neither would I make any gesture. After I had initially hailed him with the sober utterance of his name, Jacob, I merely entered his office and leaned against the jambs, like a wrench or sledge hammer laid there by a workman, and we commenced to speak, drily and without feeling, of economic and political affairs in foreign lands or the difficulties encountered by certain civil engineering projects or the desirability of a central heating system for the prison.

Gone from me now the glorious, unifying vision that had come to me with my faith when I was but a boy. Gone from me now the work of my calling, which was to make coffins. Gone from me the ways of being used in a process larger than that of my own decaying body's, gone from me the affectionate need of the community. Gone from me now even the need of my brethren in the faith, for not enough of them had followed to where I had been led, and then only a few had known, until this account, my reasons for having forsaken death and clung to imprisonment. And gone from me the urgent presence of my five children, their wonderings, their desires and needs that the incomprehensible be made comprehensible. And now, now, gone the cleaving presence and trust of my wife, for she more than any other person, except for me myself, knew now of my weakness and the state to which I had fallen. And finally, of greatest significance, gone from me the dead, gone timelessness, gone its continuous flow of wisdom, gone its absolute clarity. Gone from me now was I myself, and all that remained were the hard bright surfaces of a self that generated no light but merely reflected back whatever surfaces it met. For once a man loses his connection with whatever looms forever larger than himself, he has lost himself as well. He exists solely as a nexus after that, a mere contingency, a crossroads without a place name.

So it began to appear to me that I was utterly dependent upon the nature and character of whomever I met, before I could reveal any particular nature or character of my own. Unless I could locate clues and hints as to the forms a person used to present himself and deal with other people, which clues and hints would lead me to design appropriate forms for me to present myself back to him, then I trembled all over my body, I whimpered and spoke with an uncontrollable stammer, I fairly well wept with terror. For I had become the man of time. I had lost myself, and lost, I moved in a found world, a very real place that was stuffed to brimming with very real and threatening human beings, animals, plants, powerful objects of all possible descriptions. Nothing there was then that did not fill me with terror and confusion. Though you are seen, you cannot see, and though you are heard, you cannot hear, and though others will walk along with you, you may not walk along with them. For such is the punishment made for the man who has exchanged what is absent for what he cannot avoid. (*The Book of Discipline*, iii, 30-31.)

Every day I left my cell at dawn, and affecting gaiety, strolled to the dining hall, there to sit among my fellow prisoners and exchange views and idle thoughts while eating our usual breakfast of bread and porridge. To be sure, my stance and affect were those of a game man, a courageous fellow full of wit and intelligence, yet all the while I trembled inside, all the while I guessed and hoped and tried on faces and phrases rapidly, one after the other, eagerly awaiting the click of recognition in the eyes of the man sitting at table across from me or the sleepy eyes of the bland steward handing me my meager meal across the counter or the eyes of the guard at the door as I passed out of the dining hall to the corridor and, desperate for confirmation, found myself rushing down the stairs to the office of the man I tried to think of as my brother, for he was a man I had come to know solely by means of and in the terms of my fall from faith, and it had come to me in my moral confusion of that period that if I could love my jailor, I could perhaps learn to love myself, or what at that time claimed to be myself.

Fortunately, however, this feat was not to be accomplished. Jacob Moon was a grim man and also, as I have said, most characteristically a pragmatic man. He did not smile so much as, at moments of gaiety or high mirth, he grimaced. As, for instance, when once a donkey wandered into the prison from the street and soon had lost itself in the maze of corridors and common rooms and stairways, and as it was encountered suddenly and all out of any familiar context by one prisoner after another and one guard after another, discoveries that brought one prisoner and guard after another to the chief jailor's office to report its, the donkey's, presence, soon there had gathered at the office nearly all the prisoners and all the guards and assistant jailors and staff and even a few visitors, and still one or two more prisoners trickling in to file the identical report, that there was a donkey in the prison. The atmosphere of the gathering was jovial and easy, almost that of a holiday (for it was a particularly wintry day and the event was doubtless more diverting than if the prisoners had not felt quite so confined by the snow and cold), when at once the door to the street swung open and the chief of administration for all prisons entered, and he naturally demanded to know why the entire population of the prison had gathered here before him, to which Jacob Moon in all sincerity answered that it was because an ass had come in off the street, which statement caused a long, hearty chorus of laughter from all, even from the chief of administration himself, once it had been given him to trust that no one had intended any slight to his dignity or reputation for excellence, not to say brilliance. I myself, as the wave of laughter commenced to wash over the group, had quickly looked over the sea of faces to that of my jailor, so as to determine how he would express himself, so that I could know how I wished to express myself, and I saw his somber face spread tightly into the grimace of a man who hears laughter but no joke, and immediately I formed my face similarly. Not, I hasten to add, before I had first studied the face of the chief of administration, to be positive that he had heard and accepted the joke good naturedly.

By so great a distance was I by then lost from my old forthright self, the man who once had defied the might of the justices of this land, who had let himself be set up as an example for his brethren, so that they would know how to resist the coming pressure against their faith, by so great a distance had I drifted from that man, that I now slinked invisibly through a crowd of laughing men before I myself dared merely to let even a grimace modelled after my jailor's grimace cross my face and thus allowed myself, disguised, to join them. I was like a jackal lurking at the edge of darkness, just beyond the circle of firelight, sneaking around that edge, always peering in but always taking cowardly care never to be seen itself.

Guilt is not so much the cause of such aberrant obsequiousness and affectation as it is the result of a prior loss of unity. It is the rip in the fabric of the carefully, deliberately woven spirit of the man of faith that occurs when he misplaces or weakly gives up his faith. Where before there was a whole, a unity, there are suddenly two separated pieces, two distinct cells, and then where there were two, there are suddenly four, then eight, and so on, as the man stumbles through blocks of time, dividing and sub-dividing like an amoeba drifting through a pool of stagnant water. Obsequiousness and affectation, therefore, though they characterized all my different selves at this time, took slightly different forms with each presentation, so that, with my jailor, at least in the mornings and evenings, I was dry, dour, detached, and concerned with the kinds of events that concern engineers and administrators, but with each of the several other prisoners I associated myself with I was, in one case, as giddy and silly as an adolescent fop, even dressing up as a well known actress one morning and walking through the exercise yard presenting forged autographs to some of the simpler men, and in another case, with like-minded men, I was physically tough, stoical, disciplined, and scornful of physical weakness or disability in others, and in yet another, philosophical, meditative, pursing my mind and time thoughtfully before problems in history, language and mathematics. I was not aware at the time of any particular hierarchy among these personalities, because I was not aware at the time of any hierarchy among the models, but before long I had found myself in a sufficient number of situations where two or more of these models were in dark competition for my slavish imitation, so that I could see I was responding indeed to an hierarchy among them. At the bottom were those prisoners who were the least threatening to me physically, the weak and infirm and the principled non-violent ones, and of course my wife and her cousin Gina, and just above that level were the prisoners whose physical violence seemed to be structured on certain principles of self-defense, which made their violence somewhat predictable, and above these figures were the guards, and then the assistant jailors, and at the pinnacle, the dour figure of the chief jailor, Jacob Moon. It was with yet an additional burden of shame, then, that I came to know how utterly devoted to life had I become that I would curry favor most from those who posed the greatest threat to my life and least from those who were the least threatening to my life. I knew then that I was a lost soul, of the type that can no longer save itself but instead must be saved, if at all, by virtue of some will other than its own, which is to say, by the power of grace. I would be saved now only if the dead themselves wished it.

And so it came about that there was given to me at this time a long dream one night late in the first winter of my imprisonment, in which there spoke to me both my father and his brother my uncle, the man who had taught me my skills as a coffin-maker and who, at my father's request, had constructed my own coffin, the very one I had passed on to the saintly John Bethel some seven or eight months before. If in life we are to be touched and directed by a will other than our own, it will most likely happen while we are asleep, for sleep is as like unto death as a footrace resembles flight. Thus, in miming death, I was drawn into a passive openness to the dead and the wisdom thereof and the enactment of their will, so that my father and his brother were able to come and speak to me and I was able to hear. The encounter took place in the kitchen of the house where I had been born and raised to the time when I left and went off to live with my uncle, there to learn from him how to make coffins. My father was as he had been during my earliest childhood, very large and looming, with a broad, almost sarcastic smile, and my uncle was as he had been when I had worked with him later, my own size, solemn, bearded, and infinitely patient. We three were seated at the kitchen table, my mother was somehow present in the room but remained silent and out of sight during the interview. My father towered over my uncle and me, though we were all three seated at table as if after a pleasant meal, with dishes and cups and various implements scattered before us. Here follows the sense and direction and much of the tone of the statements given me by these two men:

Father, in a sarcastic tone signifying disapproval: We hear lately that you have allowed your attention to wander. We suppose that this is a result of some wonderful understanding you have recently come by, an understanding which supercedes our own. Perhaps you believe your new perspective unique, and if not unique, then perhaps you think it valid and ours invalid. For we, after all, are but the dead, and you are the living.

Uncle: My brother wishes to advise you, he loves you, so do not be afraid or abashed before him, merely give him your attention.

Father, angrily: He has no choice but to give me his attention! He is asleep and dreaming, and thus we have taken it from him! That is how bad a pass things have come to!

(Is this what is meant by grace? I wondered.)

Uncle: Listen to the man, he is your father, you are without wisdom, he is dead. Do not be frightened or abashed, he forgives you, he understands, you do not, he is dead and you are among the living. Fear only the living.

Father, more calmly: Fear the living, indeed. And fear even more your loss of contact with the dead. Go, return to your coffin, find yourself a gate, a wicket, and pass through it to the ground of faith that makes life endurable because honorable, honorable because honoring the dead. The coffin is your gateway. There is no other possibility for your return to honor. Expect, without it, to disappear utterly, utterly! If you will not honor the dead while you are among the living, you will be without honor yourself when you are among the dead! This is your last chance for redemption. It is your only chance for redemption.

Uncle, soothingly but with urgency: Believe him, nephew, believe him. Do not resist any longer.

Whereupon the images spun and twirled about before me, and I came awake in my cell to the glistening light of dawn, and I felt freshened in my heart, and I determined that moment to set about that very day to obtain a coffin to replace the one I had given away. I felt joy in my heart for the first time in months, and I could barely keep myself from leaping about my cell.

My first thought was that I would request my wife to search out and deliver a coffin for me, but then I realized that I would end up incriminating her and possibly some others in the crime, for such it was now, a crime. Therefore, I determined to build my own coffin in my cell and to begin the construction that very day. And when I had eaten breakfast in the dining hall, I rushed out and ran down the stairs to the chief jailor's office to request the necessary materials and tools for the building of a coffin.

For the first time in many months, as I spoke to Jacob Moon, I did not consider the manner of my being perceived. I let myself show plenty of cheek and high spirit, just as I felt it, and boldly I asked him to make certain materials and tools available to me as soon as they could

be requisitioned and delivered (it was not at all uncommon for the prisoners to request materials and tools not
unlike these, for many of them were engaged in such diverse projects as building sailboats, carving furniture and
making paneling for their cells, and other items). The list
of materials: thirty-two linear feet 1'' by 12'' pine board;
1 pint cow-glue; 2 flat steel hinges & screws for same;
6 sheets misc. grades sandpaper; 3 lbs. cotton batting; 5
yards red velvet cloth, or approx. if not available; 1 box
upholsterer's tacks; 1 quart clear varnish. The list of tools:
claw hammer; plane; square; handsaw; wood chisel;
screwdriver; sablehair paintbrush. I cannot now remember if I listed anything more, but I think this was all.

Jacob Moon, after he had read my list, directly asked
me what I wished to do with these materials and tools,
for his requisition form was required to show the proposed purpose for all such materials and tools as were
requested by prisoners or anyone else. He pointed to a
particular paragraph on the lengthy form, which did indeed assert that not to indicate thereon in detailed language the precise use to which any materials or tools
requisitioned by the office of the chief jailor from the
central supplier for all prisons, whether that use be speci-
fically for the personal deployment of the prisoners or for
prison maintenance or for the use, personal or otherwise,
of the chief jailor, was to violate the law and to be sub-
ject to dismissal and possible prosecution by the office
of the chief of prosecution. I saw, therefore, that Jacob
was merely doing his job and that he had no personal
desire or need to expose or confound me, and in fact, if
I had been willing to tell him that I wished to have these

materials and tools for the purposes of building a coffin, he would simply have filled out the requisition form appropriately and sent it on, even though he knew as well as did I myself that to request materials for the building of a coffin was to bring upon my head probable banishment from the land and possibly worse as soon as the form were received. In fact, I am sure that Jacob had not even the slightest curiosity or other interest in why I had suddenly asked for these materials and tools; he only wanted the form to be filled out as close to properly as possible.

Therefore I informed him that I did not wish to lie to him or otherwise deceive him, but I wanted to have these materials and tools for the purpose of building myself a coffin so as to pray and contemplate the dead, as I had been trained and given to do since childhood but the which in recent months had been denied me, with certain awful effects on my spirit and mind and, as I saw it, also on my destiny. I did not, however, believe that he, meaning my jailor, ought to declare on his requisition form that my purposes were as I had just described to him, for if he did so, it would doubtless go ill for him as well as for me. The offices of the chief of prosecution would think him joking, and they are not known for their enjoyment of jokes when it comes to such somber matters as the laws against worshipping the dead, and thus they would prosecute him for inappropriate levity, a mild form of heresy, to be sure, but one punishable by law none the less.

When my jailor had come fully to understand my analysis of the situation before him, he informed me that, therefore, he had only one recourse, which was to deny me my request for a requisition, and to warn me that he

was by law compelled to restrict and forbid all evidences
of worship of the dead, which meant that no coffins were
allowed inside the prison, except as required by regula-
tions of the sanitation and medical services administration
for the transportation out of the prison of the corpse of
any prisoner said to have died by infectious disease. John
Bethel, his predecessor, by his example of leniency in
these matters, had set a bad example, said Jacob Moon,
but in his later trial and punishment, had set a good example. His fate will always stand before the jailors who
follow, Jacob told me, as a clear warning of the consequence of leniency in matters concerning the laws against
the worship of the dead. For that reason, I will not permit you to build a coffin or to have one brought in here
for you by one of your secret brethren or your wife or
Gina, and I will not let you use anything as a substitute
for a proper coffin, such things as packing crates, ward-
robe closets and other such enclosures as you people in
your extremities of fervour have been known to employ,
unless, of course, you are said to have died of an infectious disease.

There was no more to be said about it. Therefore I
returned to my cell, disappointed, certainly, but full of a
strength and clarity that I had not enjoyed for months,
for now I was properly engaged with the task properly
before me, the which I had previously refused to heed, the
task of attending to the dead. I was back at the old
business of setting up the proper rites, sacraments and
artifacts, and the effects on my spirit were immediately
felt by me and manifested to everyone, so that no longer
was there any demeaning confusion over how I should

relate my divided self to the distinct, contrasting realities around me, for no longer was there any contrast between them, or them and me. I had joined them.

WHAT now follows is a description of how a great many of the imprisoned, both at my prison and at others across the land, who had no coffin came to have a coffin, and also what further was created thereby. It is, in addition, a description which must be taken as a type, revealing a type of worldly process, in the same sense that sacred scriptures are well known to reveal through types the more general events and processes.

It sometimes is forced to come out that the solution to a simple problem cannot but be complex. My problem was surely simple, that of a need to obtain a coffin, so as thereby to have followed the instructions and heeded the warnings of my beloved ancestors, instructions and warnings which, once heard, must be followed hard upon with dedicated acts of obedience. Mere suggestions and hints from the dead must be taken as absolute commands. In spiritual matters such as this, disobedience implies nothing more or less than a lack of understanding. And equally it is assumed that whoever properly understands the commands of the dead will be incapable of disobeying them. This is a necessary closure and must be accepted as such, if what is to follow will not be meaningless.

As said, my problem was a simple one. And though at first I had thought the solution would also be simple, it was not to be so. After considerable pondering upon my problem, it came to me that because Jacob Moon had been compelled to prohibit me from building my own coffin, I was now required to have one brought in to me ready-made. To be sure, he was compelled by law to prohibit me as well from importing any coffin or from utilizing any substitute as I might find among my incidental furnishings, but by disobeying him in these matters I would not, as in the former proposed solution, implicate an innocent man in my crime. I was therefore free to ignore his latter pair of prohibitions, and this thought filled me with jubilation, and I grew impatient for my wife and her cousin to arrive so that I could unfold these thoughts to them.

Upon their arrival at my cell, and after I had explained to them that henceforward I would not compel them to participate with me or with the jailor Jake (as they had come to call him) in the foul acts of sensual gratification, those spirit-soiling celebrations of life to which we had become habituated, I related to the two women the nature of my dream and the warnings and instructions I had received from my father and uncle. They both seemed greatly relieved and pleased with my obvious recovery from the disease of sensuality that had debilitated our wills for so long, and even Jacob Moon, when I had opened my experience of the dream to him, and my consequent resolution, seemed somewhat relieved and in a clear way impatient to get back downstairs to his office where, as I knew, he had a massy pile of paperwork awaiting his attention and signature. My wife's cousin, Gina, indicated that she was already late for a prior appointment in the city, and afterwards, when she had taken her leave, I related to my wife my most recent conclusion, that I was compelled by circumstance and the law to order and have shipped to me a ready-made coffin from some coffin-maker among our brethren outside.

As she is an extremely intelligent woman, she quickly pointed out to me that I would not be free to have a coffin shipped if anyone were able by examining it to determine that it was indeed a coffin, for to manufacture and distribute such items, as I more than any man must know, was a crime. In my excitement at the prospect, I had forgotten this obstacle. After a moment of dismay, however, I started up again with pleasure, for my wife suggested to me that I could surely receive a wooden cabinet or trunk, if one could be made and shipped to me, and especially if it were properly fitted out as a cabinet or trunk, so that any postal authority or prison examiner looking for contraband would, on inspecting it, conclude that the object was nothing more harmful to the common weal than a cabinet or trunk. She imaged such an object for me, pointing out that it could be made according to my specifications for a coffin, with the skin of it hinged and set with brass handles and with short legs attached to the base so as to resemble what is commonly called a hope chest and often used by young women for storing up their dowry of linens and clothing against the day when they marry (for that reason are they called hope chests). She further pointed out that it would be necessary to fill the chest with numerous items of cloth, linens, blankets and garments, &c., or the inspectors and surely my wiley jailor would discover the deceit, for they would know that I, as an impoverished prisoner, could not own sufficient items so as to require such a large chest for their storage.

This last observation by my wife, however, filled me with despair again, for I saw that no one would believe that I, of all prisoners, was the legitimate recipient of such a lavish gift as a large wooden chest filled with expensive items of cloth. My poverty was well known, for my calling had been publicly forbidden to me, and it was also well known that my wife and five children had been forced as a consequence to throw themselves upon the kindness of strangers and the few among the brethren who dared to be seen aiding them. How could a man, people would ask themselves, who cannot afford to feed and clothe and house his own wife and children, suddenly provide himself with a large hand-made wooden chest stuffed with blankets, coats, hand towels and warm undergarments?

My dear wife saw my despair and with reluctance conceded that the ruse would not be taken, though at first she had seemed to view the expense of such a gift as not especially dear or difficult to finance, even. By so much was she conscious of my need that she had difficulty making herself aware of the practical considerations. But I had swiftly itemized for her clarification the costs of such a chest and its necessary contents, as I knew any inspector would be able to do immediately upon opening it and examining it for contraband, an itemization, in fact, he would be required by law to make, so as to fix the shipping and delivery charges, and then she realized how incriminating (of me, my presumed poverty) it would be. It would be as if a starving mouse were suddenly revealed to own a cupboard full of cheese, she lightly said to me, in a characteristically generous attempt to dispel my gloom with humor.

It here came to me that the gift of the hope chest would have to be made by someone of means, if it were to be a believable gift, and such a person would have to be a philanthropist who had determined to aid and comfort those who, among society's less fortunate creatures, had been designated by society as its prisoners. Now since there was no way to regard me as worthy of being singled out by such a benefactor, for there were many who were as needy as I and some even more so, then the gift of a hope chest would have to be made to many prisoners equally and at once, enough of them so that I would not seem to have been specially chosen for the gift. The only number of prisoners that seemed appropriate, however, was three hundred eighty-seven, which was the number of prisoners, including me, then inhabiting my particular prison. I very quickly calculated what this would mean, in terms of materials alone, so as to estimate the approximate cost of such a huge undertaking as the manufacture of three hundred eighty-seven hope chests, and to my disappointment, I determined that the project would require over a half-ton of cotton batting (one thousand one hundred sixty-one pounds, to be exact), and also one thousand nine hundred thirty-five yards of red velvet cloth, and over two and one-third linear miles of twelve by one inch pine board.

At my recital of these quantities, my wife gave a high laugh and turned away from me, as if to hide tears of discouragement, for I knew that she could not imagine any benefactor wealthy enough to be willing to pay for such an undertaking. And we both knew that we could not request the gift of these hope chests and their contents from my impoverished brethren, my fellow coffin-makers who were now so scattered in the land as to be hopelessly out of contact with one another and quite incapable of a cooperative endeavor of these proportions, even had we been able to pay for the materials ourselves.

I then resolved that the cost of the hope chests and the contents therein might be borne by those wealthy citizens who seemed frequently to be willing, when properly approached, to finance the causes of the under-privileged among them, a surprisingly large group of ladies and gentlemen who, when they believe that most of the fashionable others in their class are supporting a particular cause, will themselves support that cause without question or stint. What was needed were a group of money collectors, a person able to arrange the appropriate publicity, an accountant or two to attend to the financial details and to keep scrupulous track of all funds, also an attorney, secretaries, an office of some sort, an executive director, and a board of directors. And we would need these people and facilities in the reverse order of their naming, for, once we had invited several prominent phil-anthropists to serve on our board of directors, which in-vitation, by the flattery of being singled out, they would eagerly accept, we would then be able to hire an execu-tive director at a salary consistent with his or her respon-sibilities, and once we had hired an executive director, we would be able to hire the necessary secretarial help to take care of the paperwork that would commence to arrive once the newly hired attorney had filed for the incorporation charter and with it the plea for exemption from taxation, which would not be granted by the tax

authority, of course, until we had procured the services
of several accountants and clerks so as to keep our records
in a satisfactory way, at which point we would be ready
to hire the publicist, and as soon as he or she had begun
his or her work, we would hire a battalion of collectors
to begin calling on the numerous individuals who wished
to support our particular cause.

My wife now grew exceedingly excited, and she showed
me that the most important link in this chain was the post
of executive director, for that person would be required
not only to arrange and bear the responsibility for all the
contributions coming in, but also for all the expenditures,
the half-ton of cotton batting, the two and one-third miles
of pine board, the thousands of yards of red velvet cloth,
and the purchase of the blankets, linens, clothing, &c.,
and also that person would bear the responsibility of let-
ting out the contracts to the numerous cabinet makers and
woodworkers for the manufacture of our three hundred
eighty-seven hope chests, a tedious task and one that could
only be performed by someone close to me, so that it could
be guaranteed that my specifications for the hope chest
would be followed exactly.

Who could such a person be? we asked ourselves. My
wife did not think that she would be incapable of the job,
but I disagreed, for it did seem to me that, because of
her longtime association with me and my heresy, it might
be thought by the philanthropists, if she were the titular
head of the organization, that they were coming out in
support of my particular crime of heresy. No, I told her,
they would not wish to have their endorsement of the
cause of benevolence towards prisoners in general be con-

strued as supporting any crime or prisoner in particular. And besides, I said to her, you are frail and weakly, and the demands of such a position would be beyond your capacities. She protested nobly, but I was eventually able to convince her of the foolhardiness of her desire to place herself in that position, however well-intended that desire. Next we considered her cousin Gina for the post, but again, I argued persuasively that Gina's association with the crime for which I had been imprisoned was almost as close as my wife's, especially since she had been coming to visit only me and no other prisoner for these last several months. We also considered several among the brethren who had not been imprisoned or who were not in any way known for their past or present practice of the various rites associated with our faith, but these too we had to dismiss, for the obvious reason that to organize and operate a philanthropic organization such as we were proposing would be to rip into shreds the careful fabric of invisibility that the brethren had woven in the last year. And naturally there was no imaginable way for me myself, condemned and immobilized as I then was, to direct the soliciting of funds and the expenditure thereof. And so, by gradual degrees, I began again to slip into despondency.

But I was not to remain despondent, for it shortly occurred to my wife to suggest to me the name of Jacob Moon, and immediately the gloom lifted and all was clear and bright again. For Jacob Moon was the perfect man for the job, and he would think so quite as much as we, I assured my wife. The responsibilities and tasks such a post would place before him would not leave him gaping in awe or trembling with unsureness. Jacob Moon was a man of the world, and though in a certain way, because he was so much a man of the world, I pitied him, still and all, it gave him a definite facility for working efficiently and effectively in the world. He was a living demonstration of the only aspect of being a man of time that could in any way be rationalized as a benefit of that condition, for while it is not true that every man who is able to function efficiently and effectively in the world is, ipso facto, not a man of the eternal dead, it never the less is true that every man of time, if he does not agonize over his condition and fight against it, will turn out eventually to be one of our nation's fine administrators, technicians or government functionaries. These people, because they cannot trust to luck or fate or to any of the various forces that transcend their own mortal lives, are forced thereby early in life to cultivate and refine to an amazing degree their skills and the quality of their attention to the ways of the world, with the result that they often become the men and women who are great in the eyes of the world. Only the dead, and those who worship the dead, do not envy them. The scripture says, Envy not the living. Cast not your eyes with longing upon their heaped up wealth and worldly honors, for they are but the wages of inattention to the dead, the fruits of a season lived as if it were endless. (*I Trib.*, ix, 9.) And (*I Trib.*, xxii, 30): Look unto the heavens, and let your feet fall where they may. Whether the road be smooth or rocky matters not to them, nor should it matter to you.

Thus there got created, one afternoon during the first winter of my confinement, the organization that later

became known as the Society Of Prisoners, which now
employs thousands of collectors, clerks, attorneys, secretaries, assistant directors and directors, the organization
responsible for the physical aid and comfort of millions
of our citizens (not just the prisoners, who will soon receive their hope chests, but also the manufacturers of
hope chests and the hundreds of purveyors of blankets,
linens, and clothing, &c.) It is the organization that has
come to own and manage large blocks of real estate and
public bonds and which has recently funded chairs in the
field of prison administration at several of the most pres-
tigious universities in the land. And presiding over all
this vast enterprise is the remarkable man, Mister Jacob
Moon, who once was my jailor and, in a sense, my
brother. My wife's cousin Gina is also an executive in
the Society Of Prisoners, for her special skills were required by Jacob Moon hard upon its founding, and even
my wife for a brief period was employed by SOP (as
the journalists came to call it), albeit in a relatively menial
position. Though her later illness and death, which, along
with the spiritual clarities it provided her and our children
and provided me as well, I will soon describe, prevented
her from remaining at Jacob Moon's and her cousin's
sides for long, even so, her salary and later her disability
pension were more than adequate for the support of her
and our children during the period of their greatest need.
So while I do not envy Jacob Moon or any of those men
and women whose association with the Society Of Prisoners has brought them wealth and worldly power, nevertheless, because it is not expressly forbidden by the dead,
I am grateful to them. And, of course and most important-

ly, I am grateful to them for their enormous effort to make my coffin available to me at the time of my greatest need. Gratitude is a polite form of inattention, we are taught. It corrupteth not.

I was not, however, to come to possess my own coffin for a certain lengthy period of time, which delay came as a result of the numerous obstacles to be surmounted before the Society Of Prisoners could first be set up to function properly, many of which obstacles had been anticipated by my wife and me in the conversation recorded above, but a small number there remained that we had not anticipated and that were due to shortages and other market fluctuations in the nation during those years, and thus encouraged great delay in the delivery of the actual hope chests to the prisoners. During this period of waiting, I languished in many ways as a man of time, though not so much as before, when I had not yet been visited upon in my dream of my father and my uncle and was slinking hopelessly through my days in wickedness and obsequiousness and affectation. For while it had not been difficult for me to change my behavior, such of it as could be observed by another, the difficulty came when I needed to make changes such as no one but I and the dead could see. And the behavior in particular that I came to have to labor over, in order to change myself from being a man of time to a man of the dead, was the desire that springs from memory.

This desire, sometimes called nostalgia, as such is by many overlooked and is by them regarded as of little significance morally or legally. Also, there are people who even go so far as to cultivate the appetite, to encourage the growth of those desires that have set their tap root in the soil of the remembered past. The man who worships the timeless dead, however, cannot be one of these people. He cannot condone the desire called nostalgia, and he cannot regard it as of little significance, for its presence is a sign of his fallen state. Nor can he under any circumstances actually cultivate that kind of attention. But be warned: the desire that springs from memory can trap all but the most wary of believers, and whosoever finds himself trapped, he is no longer a believer. (*The Book of Discipline*, ii, 23.)

Nostalgia comes upon a man's spirit in as many forms as the weather, blithely as a summer breeze that opens his mind to an afternoon one summer long ago when he felt at deep peace with himself, or stormily, as when a sudden violent awareness of the meaning of death sweeps over him and his mind gets crudely yanked back to another moment in time some years ago when he experienced a similarly violent awareness of the meaning of death. Or it can come like the fog, in silence and almost without his knowing, for then it will not come forthrightly as a form of memory but as something else, as a pure and particularized desire, a direct and focused appetite.

Few of us cannot recognize nostalgia in its blithe form, as simply itself, easy to dismiss as being of little consequence morally or legally. It appears innocent, to be sure, but it is not, so it is providential that what is easy to dismiss is also easy to identify, and for this reason it is only the common mind that gets tripped and trapped here. More difficult to recognize as nostalgia might be the more stormy of the two forms, but to encourage it, one must first determine whether the memory is of a pleasant sort or not, and the pause such a decision requires often exposes the trap. But many even among the most wary do not recognize nostalgia when it comes in like the fog, auguring a clear day but in fact leading in a month of rain. That is desire disguised as pure desire and not itself, which is the desire that springs from memory and which characterizes the man of time. There came a time in my imprisonment when I myself was so entrapped, when I mistook one desire for another and thus was unable to break free of time. Here is how it happened to me.

It began when I grew weary of the stale and flat food that was served up to the prisoners who had not the means to purchase their own victuals from caterers outside the prison. This daily fare of porridge and hard bread in the morning, potato soup at midday, and chickenbacks and rice in the evening, served up relentlessly without variety in the menu, soon caused me to gripe among the other prisoners, for it was a favorite topic of conversation with them, and since I wished to engage in cheerful and sociable talk with them, I was drawn to talk in a similarly complaining manner about the food. I had not noticed that the food was especially worthy of complaint until I had begun to complain of it, when, as if to confirm the reality that my words seemed to describe, I began to peer skeptically into the porridge pot in the morning and groan aloud or to smell the potato soup being prepared and shake my head and mutter bitterly, or in the evening to look to the ceiling with dismay when the attendant shoved my plate of rice and chickenback across the counter to me.

So it was that my complaint about the food, though it had commenced as a social activity, soon had validated itself against the physical surround, and thus strengthened, had taken on an obsessive and energetic quality that was matched by the complaints of only the most disgruntled and epicurean among my fellow prisoners. I was not at this time aware of my having joined these fellows in their distraction, of course, but even if I had been, I do not think I would have resisted, for a process had been set in motion that would not be ended until I had been able to turn my attention back once more to the proper contemplation of the eternal dead, who never hunger after variety or epicurean delight. The reason for this persistence of mine in complaining about the food, I then believed, was my desire, pure and simple, for varied and delightful food, and often at night while I lay in my cot and listened to the coughing, wheezing, murmuring sounds of my fellow prisoners in the darkness, I would image to myself a breakfast of fresh chilled melon, followed by a platter of shad roe and poached eggs, with hot crusty cloverleaf rolls and a pot of pure mountain-grown coffee, or a lunch of delicately flavored conch soup, fresh broiled trout and chilled white wine, with a key lime pie for dessert, or an evening meal that began with cold split pea soup with mint, cabbage in white wine, wild rice with mushrooms, a deep green spinach salad with vinegar and oil and subtle herbs, and a crown roast of pork with sausage-apple stuffing, and a cold orange souffle as a dessert. My mouth would fill with water at these images as they paraded past, one exquisitely arranged meal after another, glistening and aromatic, but soon I would topple from this pinnacle of wavering, transparent and transitory delight and would fall into a contracting pit that began with dissatisfaction, passed through resentment, and ended with gloom.

Night followed night, and so too did my longings continue unabated, evoking each night a fresh cycle of foods that I could not have, leaving me, as a result, gnashing and groveling at the bottom of my pit in frustration and gloom. Sometimes I imaged to myself only light and delicate, pastel-hued meals, fresh fruits and vegetables and thinly sliced meats, and the next night would come a menu of heavy, succulent, roughly flavored foods, to be followed the next night by a variety of casseroles and sauces, and so on, with all the accompanying greens, appetizers, desserts, breads and pastries, with all the appropriate wines, and lingering after-dinner platters of cheeses and chilled fruit and clarifying liqueurs. My desire seemed to me endless, bottomless, infinite. But so too seemed my frustration, and thus there came those moments at the gray beginnings of dawn when, questioning the legitimacy of my desire, I dragged it out before me and tried to upbraid it for causing me such sleepless frustration and gloom, and I would find myself unexpectedly defending my desire, arguing that it was endless, bottomless, eternal, asserting that thus my attachment to it was but an expression of a growing freedom from time.

This was a cruel rationalization that was but a subtle

means of sustaining my desire, of feeding it like some kind
of parasite that had attached itself to the interior wall
of my gut. But I did not understand this at the time,
because I was weak and out of contact with the voices
of the dead, for I had not my coffin at this time. My
dreams were silent, and I had no voice but my own to
advise me, and whatever construction I could put upon
the scriptures that yet rang in my head, and while my
own voice told me in consoling terms that my desire
was a natural one for a man who had been cast away in
prison, the scriptures, or so did I construe them, told me
that the appetite that cannot be sated, the longing that
knows no end, the desire that feeds only on itself, these
are but a few of the many paths out of time. Anywhere,
so long as it is out of this world! cries the prophet Walter
(vi, 12). So I reminded myself, and thus, at the bottom
of my pit of longing, would I raise up my head and listen,
and soon a consoling peace would come over me, and I
would sleep.

For several months did this circle turn in me, of complaint followed by longings which evoked glittering
images followed in turn by gloom which I nightly escaped
by rationalization and misconstrued scripture. It was in
the early spring, when I had been imprisoned for almost
a full year, which at that time seemed a great long while
to me, that several unexpected events occurred. Most men
and women who are not of our faith would not regard
them as events, but that is of no importance here. For
events are what they were, and what follows is how I understood them then. Though I will reveal shortly how I
eventually came to understand them, through the guid-

ance of the dead, for now, so that my trials and tribulation can be better grasped by the reader, let me withhold my later comprehension until I come to describe its fortunate arrival.

The first event was simply that I noticed one night while I lay in my cot and conjured images of loaded boards of steaming food, before I had come to the part in my nightly sequence when I began the quick slide into despair, I realized that the feast set before me was one I had already imagined, was a meal I had conjured several months earlier. This came upon me first as a surprise, for I had thought the menu could be infinitely varied, and then as a disappointment, for immediately the image of the meal seemed less succulent, less attractive, less necessary than before, and my mouth did not fill with water quite as before. I did not understand this diminishment of my desire, and somewhat fuddled, I tried again, and I sent the broiled trout back to the kitchen, as it were, as if the waiter had made a terrible mistake, and ordered again, this time a crispy roast pig stuffed with apples and sausage. But this meal too was familiar to me, for it too had I earlier brought forth from my imagination (for there did I then believe these images to emanate from). Again I returned the meal to the kitchen and called for another, barbecued swordfish, but this too, when it appeared steaming in its juices before me, I saw I had already ordered once, and thus it went sailing back to the chef, who by now must have been close to despair himself. On it went, one after another, until I began to grow shrill and wild, ordering rapidly and without care.

Suddenly, as if to quiet me for a moment while the poor

harried chef struggled to assemble his masterpiece, there was set before me a glass and a dark bottle of twenty year old port wine. I poured a glassful, raised it and with my eyes praised the regal hue of the wine, sniffed it with pleasure, and let it into my mouth. This was the second event. For it was as if the wine had replaced the banquet of before, and instantly my earlier endless desire for delicious and various foods had been replaced by a new endless desire, this one for fine wines, hearty whiskeys, froth-topped ales and sharp tangy liqueurs and brandies that heat the chest. In my mind I drank off the bottle of port wine, and as soon as it was emptied, I tumbled as before into my pit of despondency, where I nursed myself with consoling rationalizations concerning the spiritual quality of my desire and with scripture appropriated and translated for my own greedy use.

The next night I requested a brilliant beaujolais, and then the following night a chablis from an obscure but old and honorable vineyard, and then, one night after another, one excellent old wine after another, until it occurred to me that a peaty ten year old whiskey from the north would be pleasant, and then a bottle of cognac, a coffee brandy from the tropics, a rice wine from the orient, a powerful honey liqueur, a pale and breathtaking rum, and on and on, long careful solitary nights at table as I raised glass after glass to the light, admired the color and texture, brought the glass to my lips, and while it still quivered there, suddenly plummeted into the pit of frustration, resentment, gloom, there to anesthetize my pain with specious argument and misapplied scripture.

So it was that I did also complain as before among my

fellow prisoners when at leisure or at table, except that now I whined about the prohibitions against alcoholic beverages and other intoxicants, and that now the prisoners among whom I gathered to complain were the swollen-bellied addicts of alcohol, the slaves to gin, the nervous red-nosed lovers of whiskey and rum, the bleary-eyed connoisseurs of wine. No longer were my consorts the epicureans with their jowls and gout, the feasters and thick-lipped lovers of dripping chunks of flesh and all the fastidious gourmets of my small society. To exchange one group of complainers for another, however, was merely to rattle the chain that bound me, though I did not realize that then. I believed instead that I had moved from a dull group of misanthropic associates to a group more responsive and sensitive to my spiritual quest. Such was the extent of my delusion, the degree of my depravity. And so it was that by night I conjured images that eased my hungers and slaked my thirst without releasing me from either, while by day I sourly studied and discussed prohibitions and limits without attempting to transcend or overleap them.

I do not know how long, as my condition, this would have gone on, or if in the end I would have profaned myself utterly and turned irreconcilably away from the dead, had I not one night exhausted the inventory of wines, whiskeys, brandies, liqueurs and ales that were available to me and had I not, while wildly sending back each new bottle as it appeared to me, suddenly been distracted by the image of money. Be not astonished by this, for someday you too may find yourself in a similar trap, and then may you recall that after the desire for food comes the desire for drink, and after the desire for drink comes the desire for money, cash, coins, currencies of all nations, bullion, personal checks, bank checks, refunds, all forms of money, one after the other, in bound stacks, in high trembling columns, in glimmering solid bricks, in all the forms that you have ever seen. Oh, what chests of money I had hauled out, what safe deposit boxes, what caches and stashes I rifled and gloated over during those long summer nights! What great good fortune suddenly would shower me with riches, coins of all realms falling through my fingers, bills stuffed into all my pockets, my wallet bulging like a thick mackerel in my hand, while I lay there in my cot in the darkness of my cell, counting on into the night, tens, hundreds, thousands, millions of dollars and cents, pounds, pesos, francs, marks, pesetas, reals, ruples, yen, lira, and on and on, as if the numbers were able to run endlessly on all the way to infinity.

Precisely as I had before, I moved to a new link in the chain that bound me, turning my backside to my former friends, the lovers of drink, so that I could complain alongside those who were poor, those who resented the wealth of certain individuals among us or the wealth of the jailor and his assistants, who, by bribery and other emoluments, had managed to supplement their salaries quite handsomely, and even resented the wealth of the citizens who remained outside the prison and whom we never saw but still remembered. Thus, as before, my days were spent with all my attention directed bitterly to the limits that bound me, and my nights were spent in vain fantasies that those limits did not exist, with the inevitable collapse against the unavoidable knowledge that they did truly exist, and the last self-solacing whimpers at dawn that this terrible cycle somehow expanded my spirit.

Oh, foolish, deluded, self-profaning man of time! What will save you from yourself? What will turn you away from this pathetic ferreting about? Must you count all the money in the world, all the dollars and all the cents, all the bills and coins ever issued by all the treasuries in the histories of nations, before you can see the truth? Must you exhaust all the finite inventories in the universe, and still go on longing, before you realize what it is that you long for? Do you not know that while you are counting, still counting, long before you have neared the end even of this finite set, death will come and take you, and everything will have been for nought, for zero, as if you had never counted the monad that all along stared you in the face?

These are the questions that came to me, then, one slow word at a time, until it appeared to me that the chain I was forging was itself endless and that it could go on longer than I could. For while it is the chain of delusion itself that is infinite, my own delusion was that each finite link was infinite. Had I possessed my coffin during those months of my vain desires, I surely would have seen that each set of desires was a finite set, for I would have seen, as I see now, that each set depended on my personal memories of food and drink and monies in order for me to image any particular member of that set. And when I had seen, by virtue of the grace sacrament provides, that I had been all along experiencing nothing more than the desire that springs from memory, no twisting of scripture would have worked for me to excuse myself. Thus armed, I would have steeled myself against the desire by denigrating the memory and then by turning all my attention to the further contemplation of the dead, who have no memory.

But without my coffin, without access thereby to the sacrament that could have provided grace with ease, I was forced to lengthen the cycle, to add link to link, until at last, no matter how I squirmed and wriggled, I could not deny the evidence that all the links would be the same and endlessly, and that all I was about during these complaining days and dreaming nights was the business of binding myself into time. It was a discovery made possible by intellect, rather than by rite, but it was no less gratuitous for that and thus no less an aspect of the grace that flows from the dead. I fell on my knees, as I do now, and I thanked the unruffled, objective, endlessly uninvolved dead for the freedom to think clearly and thereby to free myself from the bondage of the finite, the chain of life, the links of the desire that springs from memory.

This episode in my spiritual growth marked the end of my weakness for nostalgia. By cleansing myself of my desires for varieties of food, for varieties of drink, and for endless numbers of money, I cleansed myself of the taint of nostalgia. And thus was my growth allowed to continue, where before it had been impeded and had even been thrown backwards so to create a diminishment. It was a painful period in my life, and often a bewildering one, but all that was to make my ultimate freedom from it the more victorious and exemplary.

OR reasons at first unknown to me, when I was falling regularly into disputes with those prisoners who previously had joined me daily in my complainings, I felt compelled to blame myself. Later I saw that my reasons were natural if not well-founded, for as much as I had made myself come forward after months, even up to a year or possibly more, of complaining and then dreaming and then making specious argument, by that same distance as I had come forward was I regarded by my old associates with mistrust. Now, this is in the nature of things, that when a companion comes forward and leaves you behind, you will bridle at him when he speaks to you and attempts to bring you forward also to stand beside him. You will try to argue that he has fallen away, and he will argue that he has come forward, and so the two of you will fall into dispute.

It was not wholly a legitimate thing for me to do, then, when I proceeded so quickly to blame myself for the disputes, but after all, I was the one who had moved out of step, and I could not think of my movement except as a forward one, and so naturally I could not help but attempt to convince my fellow prisoners to follow me to that place, which place I knew was no more than a quickstep nearer to death. Yet all the same, I knew that if I had not tried so diligently to bring my fellow prisoners to a deeper understanding of the worship of the dead, there would not have been those painful, sometimes frightening disputes and arguments and the numerous sudden flights of irritation. My companions did not want me to leave them, whether by means of a step forward or of a falling away, but once I had done so, they did not want me to try to take them with me.

Yet I had no choice in the matter. It was my calling to make coffins to aid in the further worship of the dead, and in the absence of conditions which would make that activity possible, in order still to practice my calling I was obliged to draw others unto the dead in whatever ways there were available to me, and in this case, at this time, the only means available to me was argument. And so, whenever possible, I met my fellow prisoners with argument and deep reasoning, with intent talk and formal challenge and with careful discussion, bringing my own most complicated and subtle thoughts to bear on the question of the proper place for a human being's attention, and in the process drawing forth from my fellows their most complicated and subtle thoughts on the question. Thus, if I could not make my fellows a coffin, I would make them some deep and thrilling argument instead. If I could not work for the dead in one way, I would do it in another.

The first of my previous companions to grow weary of my company and to show it to me were those who in the previous winter had got me to dress myself up as a famous actress and go about in the exercise yard where there were many of the simpler prisoners and offer them my autograph, which they excitedly accepted and soon were squabbling over amongst themselves, to the lasting amusement of my companions and also to me at that time, although later it seemed to me a pointless and even slightly cruel thing to do, and I was ashamed of myself for having done it. But after I had gone through my long winter and spring of complaining and griping and fantasizing and rationalizing, and eventually had come to know myself in this matter, then I could no longer join these fellows in their play and their jokes on the other prisoners. I was forced to refuse them on several occasions, first when they came to me and invited me to join them in their attempt to trick up some of the exercise equipment in the gymnasium so that the bigger, athletic men would be likely to fall and hurt themselves when they began to exercise, and then a few weeks later when they wanted me to help them decorate the dining hall for a Mayday masquerade party. I thought both activities wrong headed, the first because it would cause unnecessary anger and possible injury and the second because the celebration of the first day of the month of May was a deliberate carry over from the days when it had not yet been thought of to worship the dead and men and women went around year after year making holidays out of seasonal and celestial cycles and changes which they foolishly associated with the patterns and needs of their own mortal lives. The amnesty associated with the solstice and applied every year to the short-term prisoners and the tried and convicted political and religious offenders willing to sue out a pardon, as they called it, was a celebration of this type. Possibly this amnesty was one of the reasons why Mayday, too, was regarded as such a significant holiday in the prison. I could not say for sure, but when I offered my reasons, as described above, for not wishing to participate in the preparations for the masquerade party associated with the holiday, I was told by one of the celebrants that soon the amnesty would be made, and then all the prisoners in his group, and here he waved his hand in a circle to indicate to me his many friends, would be gone out of prison and would be lost to one another forever. Some of them even had wives, he said to me, as if this were a sad thing, and many of them would be obliged to go back and make their residences far from one another all across the nation. Thus, he said, Mayday was an important holiday for them.

I could feel a certain sympathy for them. It was true that most of this particular group of prisoners would indeed be affected by the workings of the amnesty at the solstice, for most of them, as it turned out, had been confined for political reasons, in so far as the manner of their affection for men and their preference for the company of a man to the company of a woman were to be understood as crimes against the state. For indeed, when the continued good health of the state is economically dependent upon the family and upon sexual unions therein between a man and a woman, to withhold oneself from participating with eagerness in such a union is to undermine the very foundations of the state. Though I myself was not guilty of this particular crime, I was, however, guilty of a crime similarly identified, and for that reason I felt a special kinship with these surprisingly good-natured fellows. I say surprisingly because I knew how much they had suffered for their predilections and derelictions, and it would have been a reasonable thing for them to have been far more bitter and belligerent towards those of us who were not of their particular persuasion as regards the family or as regards copulation with women. (Many of them, in confidence, did tell me that they often had copulated with women and in fact were very fond of the company of women, even more than was I myself. I found this hard to understand. Actually, I found it hard to believe, and that is what I found hard to understand, for why should I not believe what I am told by a man I do not hold to be a liar?)

They made no particular protest to my refusal to join them in their tricking out the exercise machines, even when I volunteered my reasons for not wishing to join them, which were, as I said, because I feared it would cause unnecessary anger and possible injury. I added that the taking of one's pleasure from any increase in the quantity of anger in this already steaming world was inattentive to the teachings of the dead, and here I showed them from *The Book of Tribulations* (xi, 13) that the man who cultivates anger cultivates a desert. But they heard me not, and heard not the words of the dead, and instead went laughing away from me and set about to arrange the exercise machines so that several of the machines did indeed break with malicious force as soon as they were used, and as I had predicted, this caused a significant amount of anger, which did not seem to dismay my friends in the least, and also caused one rather cruel injury to the groin of one of the men caught in a tricked-out machine, which injury did not sadden any of my friends, at least in no way that I could determine.

When a few weeks later they came back to me and tried to convince me to join them in making their decorations of the dining hall for the purposes of the masquerade party associated with Mayday, they were more persistent than before, the which persistence I credited to the fact that as a coffin-maker I was known to be a clever man with tools and certain of their plans were sufficiently elaborate that they required the aid of people who were clever with tools. So when I refused them and gave them my reasons, which I have already described and will not say over again here, they were irritated with me and fell into arguing heatedly with me, some of them, while others tried cajoling me, while yet others promised rewards and certain unnameable services in return for my help. But I resisted them all. To their arguments I responded with counterarguments, which I fortified and validated with scripture, so that before long it was clear to everyone that all they had to present on their side was merely the argument of justification by sentiment, whereas mine was the argument of justification by metaphysic, and when I had pointed this out and had reminded them of the hierarchy among forms of argument, they were silenced, though I fear they were not convinced. To those who tried cajoling me with their high spirits and jokes and the promise of hearty fellowship, urging me to go along with the group because not to do so would leave me in a solitary way, I responded that without the dead I am forever in a solitary way and with the dead I am never alone. This also was successful in silencing them, and their cajoling ceased directly, and they too went off from me, leaving only those few who were making promises of unnameable services to me in return for my helping with the decorations, which help involved the construction of a garlanded and festooned temple in the middle of the dining hall, along with some machinery and stages for certain proposed theatrical and musical productions. To these last among my former companions, I said that I had turned my attention away from the living and toward the dead and that I was therefore striving mightily not to be a man of time any longer, which meant that such sensual pleasures as they promised were meaningless to me at best and corrupting to me at worst. Therefore, said I, to offer me a meaningless pleasure is to offer me no pleasure at all. It is to offer only confusion, guilt and fretfulness, for which I would not be able to thank you, for which, in fact, I would virtually resent you. No, said I, the service shall be mine, and that service is to refuse you, so that I will not resent you. But this did not please them as I had hoped it would, and with several blatant shows of their disgust and incomprehension, they departed from me.

Another group of men with whom I fell frequently into dispute were the athletic men, most of whom were committed to violence, I admit, but who only opened themselves to its use in a principled way, in comparison with the several madmen and the dozen or so youths who saw violence more or less as a symbol for something else (rather than the more usual opposite way of regarding it). These the madmen and the flighty youths with knives and other honed bits of metal that they secreted in divers parts of their bodies and clothing, these were a type I did not dare dispute with. I confess it now, even though

I know that had I then my own coffin to which I could have resorted for strength and wisdom every evening, I surely would have dared to confront these madmen and youths who are, every time they are seen, in a wild chase for anyone who would obstruct or hinder them, and the one who would do so would get mashed up by them, for it is the mashing that they love. They often chased after me to obstruct or hinder them, but I would not, despite their attempts to force me by making outrageous demands upon me. For without my coffin, no matter how elevated and rigorous my attempts to transcend the limits of my mortal structure, I was never the less in this respect, in the respect of my physical cowardice when faced by a madman or a gang of wild-eyed youths trying to make themselves secure by committing acts of violence, still a man of time.

It was not so difficult for me to stand and bring forth argument with the athletes, though, those hulky, bulky men who lifted enormous weights and exercised for long hours every day and even at night, for I knew that, regardless of their commitment to and enjoyment of certain acts of violence against other human beings, it was under the guidance of principles of self-defense and was thus predictable. They relished and told long stories of mighty bouts, recounted great bone-crunching episodes of violence, but all their stories and accounts were guided by the wish to point up the principle of self-defense, its necessity, utility and justification, almost as if they were telling little fables or parables designed to say the virtue of their authors' lives of heavy discipline, their lives of contrived restraint. And of course, because they tended to be much larger than most men and much stronger and more skilled in the ways of breaking bones and tearing muscle and rupturing organs and various membranes, they also tended to regard the granting of protection as closer to the act of grace than they did the actual perpetrating of violence on the body of someone smaller, weaker or less skilled than they. Instinctively, almost, they knew that if they withheld their great power, they would be exercising the greater power, for grace, which is always gratuitous, functions essentially to dignify and glorify the dispenser. It is self-redounding, and for that reason whether it is utilized by the recipient or not matters not a whit to the dispenser.

Over the course of my first year of imprisonment I had often been placed under the protection of one or more of these men, a pure act of grace on their part, awarded to me regardless of my need or particular qualities and given out solely because they were huge and I was not, because they were skilled at various of the martial arts and I knew nothing of these, and because they were extremely strong, especially through the upper body, and I was no stronger through the upper body than any man who has spent his adolescence and young manhood as a builder of coffins. I welcomed this dispensation, naturally, for it meant a distinct falling off of the number of mean and nasty occasions during a day when I would be accosted by one of the madmen or the gangs of flighty youths out looking for someone unable to keep himself from obstructing or hindering them. I also enjoyed the companionship of these large, soberly disciplined, methodical men, and many were the mornings and late afternoons when I would descend the stairs to the exercise room, where they moved about like enormous beasts of burden in the cool, dim light, lifting barbells and cast iron weights, pulling rhythmically on thick rubber belts attached to the walls, studying their development in the mirrors that lined the room. Sometimes a pair of them would meet together on a mat and wrestle for a while, under strict rules and heavy manners, so that they would not injure one another by accident. It pleased me to stand and observe while they went through their numerous exercise programs and afterwards to listen to their conversations about bodies and physical tests of all kinds and even sometimes, especially after the spring, to discuss matters with them, such as the need to worship the dead.

Ordinarily they tolerated my argument with them, which necessarily took the form of disagreement followed by a presentation of my view only, for they did not seem to think the situation warranted their presenting their argument or point of view, and to be sure, they were not always as easy with speech as I doubtless seemed to be, for their response to my argument was usually to throw themselves grunting back into a series of exercises or to whack against the large sandbag several hundred times with their fists.

Once, however, they came to me and urged me to accept an exercise program for myself, one of their own design, and when I declined, with lengthily explained reasons, all of which were of course religious, they became quite angry and heated about it. This surprised me, but it soon came out that a particular pair of them had decided to experiment with my body because it was so approximate to the shape and condition of the body of the average citizen outside the prison, and they felt that if they could design an exercise and conditioning program which was capable of converting my somewhat flabby structure into an iron-hard, machine-like, impeccably muscled structure like theirs, then they would be able to sell their program, like a recipe for a cake to the hungry, once they were released and let back outside again. I did not see anything amiss with their plan, and I even told them this, for if indeed they had been allowed to employ my body in this testing out of their exercise program, I was sure that in time they would have come up with a series of diets, exercises, activities and sports that would have converted my structure into the kind of organism that would have evoked deep envy and marvelling from among practically all men who do not worship the dead. Then they could have come forth with descriptions and measurements of my rapid progress to physical perfection, and their program would have been eagerly purchased by untold numbers of citizens outside. It might have made my two bulky companions into rich men.

But no, I would not allow it. The body is not the temple of the worship of the dead; it is the priest's vestment, no more. To attend with any great part of one's time, energy and treasure to the care of this vestment is to leave off the proper use of it, which is merely to signify the office. For we have been granted ordination at birth, and only death can properly remove the vestment and the obligation that adheres to it. Tending to it ourselves, I told them, cultivating it, treating it as if it were some

object of worship itself, is to fall into a subtle yet dangerous form of blasphemy. Said the prophet Dirk, We wear
our bodies. They do not wear us. For while we can ignore
them, they can never ignore us. In life, it is crucial to
learn what can be ignored, and then to ignore it. For
what cannot be ignored, must be worshipped. (*Dirk*,
xxiii, 12-15.)

As it happened, then, the two who had asked it of me
that I let them use my body to exemplify the bodies
of the future purchasers of their program, these two had
up to then been my most consistent protectors against
the raids against me by the madmen and the marauding
gangs of youths, who spent much of their idle time ac-
costing the prisoners who often walked about without
any clannish loyalty from among the principled violent
ones. Unfortunately, my argument against my protectors'
plan for my body was such that it smouldered them
angrily against me, so that they withdrew their protection and talked bitterly against me among their brethren,
until there was no other protection from any of them
forthcoming.

And thus in a short time I was accosted by one of the
gangs of knife boys, and to punish me for my cowardice,
which let them pitch me around one to the other while
they laughed at me and urged me to stand and fight any
one amongst them, the leader of the group cut my skin
with his knife, not deeply enough to injure me in any
debilitating way, but sufficiently to indicate his capacity
for killing me and his deliberate withholding of that
capacity. The cuts were also deep enough to create the
scars on my face which have caused so much rumor and

confusion among my brethren. I hope now that there will be no more wild and exaggerated tales to soar about the countryside concerning the sufferings of my imprisonment. To be sure, there followed numerous other encounters with violence which were equally characterized by their unavoidability, now that my protection from the athletes and body builders had been withdrawn, and even though several of them indeed left me with injuries, none of the injuries have given rise to the type of rumor and outright lie as have done the scars on my face, so for that reason I will not ennumerate and describe them here.

Excepting the company I kept with those men among the prisoners who could be called the philosophic ones, I was now more alone than I had been since my arrival in prison the year before. This did not so much depress me as it frustrated me, for I had, in my enjoyment of the daily company of these various fellows, sought to work amongst them for their conversion to the wisdom and the ultimate salvation of the worth of a life that lay in keeping my faith and observing its sacraments. I was not capable of expressing this ambition in my dealings with the philosophic ones, however, for their conversion is not normally accomplished by their coming to know the texture and the quality of the life of a believer. No, the philosophers, though they may indeed adhere to a set of beliefs for no other reason than that they themselves once, when youthful and less taught in argument, came to know the texture and quality of the life of a man they admired, once they learn how to philosophize with those beliefs will brook no further conversions to be similarly accomplished. Thus they are seldom seekers of belief so much as they are defenders of it, and therefore, if you would attempt to work conversion on them, you must first destroy their present set of beliefs, and this, according to scripture, would be in defiance of the dead. Shatter not any man's faith if you would have him as your brother. Let him love your faith and with his love shatter his own. Make not a man naked before you present him with a cloak. (*I Craig.*, vii, 18.) In addition, I was not as clever and schooled as they generally were, and often, in explaining the nature and the principles that defined my own mode of worship and the very necessity of worship itself, I made a poor case for myself and my brethren, and I sometimes glumly conceded that I was making no sense.

So it came about that, even though these men were then my only companions among the prisoners, as I was compelled by my love of the dead and my wish to obey scripture, I left off attempting to work conversion among the philosophic ones, with the immediate result of their no longer desiring me to come among them. As long as I had been willing to argue against the faith they defended, I had been welcomed as one of their fraternity. But when I determined that by my own faith I must not attack theirs (and by that means also no longer to be forced into glum concessions of making no sense), the philosophic ones no longer found me of interest. This was to become a considerable deprivation for me, for I had learned to value the companionship of the philosophers above all others and for reasons that had nothing to do with the disputation they themselves valued so highly, and when I was no longer able to sit with them at table or in the prison reading rooms or even to play dominoes with them (for when I left off arguing against them, they no longer were able to respect my intelligence), I sat alone in my cell and wondered what they were doing at that moment, what they were saying to each other, what they were analyzing, discussing and evaluating together, for these were men who talked with feeling and intelligence about many of the things that interested me.

I did not complain then, nor do I now, even though I had fallen into a deep solitude that was broken only by the sporadic visits of my wife, who was growing more weakly, and, for a brief period, the occasional conversations I had with Jacob Moon prior to his departure from his post as jailor, which also took place that second summer of my imprisonment, when he assumed the directorship of the Society Of Prisoners. I did not complain of my solitude, first, because there was no one but my wife to hear it and I did not wish to increase her sufferings by a relation of my own, but also because I knew that my solitude had been achieved by me in the service of the dead, and so I saw my sufferings as yet another way to tender mercy to the dead, and this made me glad.

cannot now say with certainty when it was that I reached this period of my deep solitude, which goes on even to today, except to notice that it occurred sometime long before the death of my beloved wife, which means that it probably took place during the early part of the first eleven years of my imprisonment, for I am told that her death took place only a year ago this last winter. Regardless, my experience of the passage of time for those years had become over the years such that I could recall the most distant parts with great clarity and detail, almost as if they were events of barely a month ago. But as the events came nearer in time to the present moment, I found myself unable to recall them very clearly and sometimes not at all. I do not know for sure why this should be so. It is more usual that the opposite should be the case, that I should remember events of ten and twelve years ago only vaguely and with great gaps of forgotten days, with even months and whole seasons missing, and that I should remember the more recently transpired events of my imprisonment with a more reliable continuity and in much sharper and more plentiful detail.

I have studied this seeming paradox with care, especially in the absence of my coffin, to which ordinarily I would have repaired for meditation and access to a higher intelligence than my own, and I have devised a theory to explain the phenomenon. Here it is. In as much as all my efforts during my imprisonment after the loss of my coffin were bent singlemindedly toward freeing me from being the man of time who moves through tiny segmented cells of experience in time, and in so far as I did succeed in those efforts, by that much would I be freed of the burden and the incriminating stain of memory. And in so far as my success in this undertaking was marked by gradual degrees, so too would my freedom from memory be gradual and relative.

This made sense to me, and on the several occasions when I related my theory to my wife, it made sense to her as well. I had no one else to confirm or deny or even to question the validity of my theory, for, as I have described, my fellow prisoners had removed themselves from my company, setting the kind of precedent which in prison life does not easily get broken, regardless of the regular movement in and out of that society, and when my jailor Jacob Moon had departed from his post, there was no one even among the staff who was willing to associate with me either. According to my wife there were many of our brethren who wished often to visit me in my confinement, but because to do so would bring upon them certain exposure and possible prosecution, they were forced with reluctance to stay away. And even if they had wished to take such a risk, I would not have allowed it, for my best use to them was as an example, not as a companion nor even as an object for their sympathies. Also, as I mentioned, my wife's cousin Gina, who in the beginning of my imprisonment would visit me frequently, after my having been brought to my senses by the words spoken to me in my dream by my father and his brother, feared that I would only be reminded by her presence of that for which I felt considerable guilt. This I took to be an unintended but precise description of how she herself doubtless felt, and thus I urged my wife to assure her cousin that she need not visit me anymore, that in fact I would consider it unbecoming of her to do so, for I would take it as an indication that she did not herself feel any guilt for the nature of our carnal activities together in those early days of my imprisonment. My wife told me that her cousin accepted this message with her usual placid understanding, and this pleased me and gave me hope that the entire experience had enlarged her spiritual understanding of the nature of carnality and the dead as much as it had my own.

But with regard to my theory about the paradoxical way in which my memory had come to function and not to function, almost as if it had come partially to withhold itself, because there was no one against whom I could test it with argument, except my wife, of course, who agreed fully with me on most things of a theoretical nature anyhow, I was not able to be sure that I was not merely constructing an elaborate disguise so as to hide some painful truth from myself. Whenever one is unsure in this way, if he cannot resort to his coffin and there obtain his confirmation or denial, he has little choice, indeed, he is obliged to do nothing else, than to turn to scripture and hope that his confirmation or denial can be obtained there. For as the scriptures themselves say, Certainty eludes him who will not read deeply into the language of the dead. (*Craig.*, xiv, 22.) And truly, there amongst the scriptures did I find confirmation of my theory, concerning my memory's increasing ability (as I extricated myself from time and came slowly back into the proper and fitting worship of the dead) to withhold itself.

Now this my reader may think odd, for it may seem to him that I was testing and confirming a theory about the gradual loss of memory with scriptures that I had access to only by means of memory (for the possession of scripture in any printed form was strictly illegal, then as now). May it here be pointed out that my memory was not flawed or imperfect with regard to what it described to me, whether of scripture or of the nature of my experience, as much as it was increasingly absent altogether and increasingly, therefore, reported nothing to me of my experience. My memory of scripture, which I had learned when a mere child, was not affected. But whole days went by without leaving a word in my mind's report to me on myself, then whole weeks, and then months and seasons, until it was no longer my memory that told me how long I had been imprisoned or precisely when particular events had occurred, as much as it was a tattered calendar on the wall of the dining hall or a casual conversation between two prisoners overheard in the exercise yard or a newspaper in the reading room.

Thus I gradually lost my old ability to move easily among sequences of events, public and private, and my old ability to relate the two chains so that I could immediately know what public events had transpired at the same time as a given private event. There was a morning,

for example, when, upon looking into the mirror over
my wash basin, I realized that my hair had gone all to
white, where before it had been dark brown, and I cannot now say whether I made that discovery mere days
before I learned of my wife's death or seven whole
years before. And there was the period of several months
when the prisoners were talking amongst themselves of
the war that the nation was evidently prosecuting abroad,
and I cannot say whether this period was before or after
my hair had turned white. And though I can remember
the evening of resignation when I decided that I would
no longer every ninety days file an appeal for a trial
at the upcoming quarter-sessions, so that I could be tried
and properly convicted and thus be made eligible for
amnesty at the following solstice, a decision I knew was
based on the fact that I had been refused such a trial
by peremptory notice a hopelessly repeated number of
times, I cannot now say how many times I had been
refused. That is to say, I cannot now say on what numer-
ical basis I made such a momentous decision.

Doubtless there are some among the brethren who
would say that this seeming dysfunction of the memory,
even if it indeed was a direct result of my attempt to
remove myself from the life of a man of time, was a
deprivation and a kind of suffering. But I cannot agree.
For the prophet Walter says, There will come a day that
will not differ from night, and a night that will not differ
from day. (vii, 7.) No, this was not a dysfunction of the
memory. It was a more and more frequent withholding
of itself, and thus it was another of the many kinds of
grace that get granted to those who worship the dead.

And grace, as I have said, is the gift that redounds to the greater glory of the giver, and in that way does it serve its purpose. By this gift, therefore, was I permitted to see the true and overwhelming nature of the dead all the more clearly. To hear the voice of the dead is to obey it, and to see its everlastingness is to honor it. To obey death and to honor it, then, are to make the life of a man overflow with meaning. If the gradual loss of my memory, properly understood as grace, served to make my life gradually more meaningful to me, how could I call it a dysfunction? Or even more absurd, how could I call it a deprivation or a kind of suffering?

T HERE came to me a slowly dawning realization, like the spread of a thick silvery light, that my wife had left off coming to visit me in my imprisonment. For a long time her visits to my cell, where we would sometimes converse and more often would sit comfortably together for hours in affectionate silence broken only by some one or another of my thoughts or memories that I felt would be of use in her instruction, had been less and less frequent. Or so it then seemed to me, for whenever she did appear to me there, it did seem to me that I had not been in her company for a long while. As I look back now to that period of my imprisonment when I first began to notice the infrequency of her visits to my cell, I picture her as being somewhat distracted and erratic in her words, but I did not then notice that her behavior was anything out of the ordinary. I had noticed, naturally, from the very beginning of my imprisonment, even from the day of my arrest, when, because of the tumult and frenzy of those days she had been delivered too soon of the child she was then carrying and which as a consequence had died, that her health was precarious and that she was often in pain and would fall to coughing and wincing from it. Her condition worsened, and I did notice that and did advise her on how to medicate herself as best I knew how, and I did direct

her to those among the brethren who I knew could provide her, out of their love for me, with aid and comfort
and who would also stand forth in the support of our children. For this support my wife expressed often to me her
large gratitude, for she as well as I knew how dangerous
it was for them to make any show of public sympathy
for my dependents.

During those early years of my confinement, my wife
and I were at deep peace with one another and were in
continuous agreement on all the questions, quandaries
and tribulations that beset us and the numerous ways by
which we tried to answer and alleviate them. But there
came at last a season when it was known to me that no
longer was I capable of advising or otherwise aiding her
in her attempts to contend with the obstacles she faced
in the world outside my prison as she struggled to care for
herself and our children. Her knowledge of the outside
world had grown to be superior to mine. And thus I gave
off attempting to provide more than a generalized and ab-
stract reassurance, which I am sure must at times have led
her to believe or to fear that I no longer cared very deeply
about the welfare of my family and that I no longer held
for my wife the same passionate devotion as when before
I had been imprisoned. It is to this belief or fear, then,
that I credit her increasingly distracted and erratic behavior, which I did not notice at the time but from which,
if I had noticed it, I would have drawn the same conclu-
sions as now, and I would have tenderly remonstrated
with her so as to show her the constancy of my caring
about the welfare of my family and the continuity of my
devotion to her person.

This was not of course the cause of her death, any more than it was the cause of the death of my first wife, the mother of my five children, even though, according to the physicians who attended the women during their last days, they both died from the same affliction, a congenitally distressed heart, the physicians called it, worsened by the depredations of poverty and the stress of life and time. My chiefest grief is that I could not be in attendance when these two precious women passed over from their sufferings in life to their comfort in death and that, therefore, my last memories of both my wives are sombered to such a huge degree by the character and intensity of their tribulation in life rather than of their bliss in death. Thus it had been with a certain amount of envy that I had heard my first wife's father tell me how his daughter had joined the dead, for during the months of her dying I had been compelled by my calling to provide crucial training to the many in the north who wished to become coffin-makers. And it was with a similar envy that I heard my sons tell me of the dying of my second wife, their stepmother, during the winter of the eleventh year of my confinement. Here is how it came about.

My wife had not come to visit me for a long time. I could not say exactly how long, nor could I even be approximate, but I had concluded never the less that she had left off coming to the prison, and the conclusion had filled me with a kind of releasement that I did not at first understand. Since that time I have come to view that releasement, which felt to me like a thick silvery light spreading across my mind, as, first, a secret awareness that my wife at last had more satisfying things to do with her time than to sit in a tiny damp cell with me, and this gladdened and relieved me, and, secondly, as a quiet harbinger of her death. At the time, however, I did not view the presence of that light in either of these ways, I merely opened myself to it, and it was only after my two oldest sons had come and had presented themselves to me that I went back to that light and attempted to interpret it.

One of the assistant jailors, a man whose name I do not know, brought the two boys to me. The older of the pair, my firstborn, had grown into his young manhood, and I did not recognize him. The second so closely resembled his mother that at first I took him to be her in fact, and I gloried in her presence, for I knew her to have been among the dead for many years. But soon they had told me their names and had led me to understand that they were indeed my two oldest children, and we sat down together side by side on my cot and began to speak fondly to one another, albeit somewhat tensely, it seemed, for many years had passed since we had been in each other's company and we were all three not sure of how best to make ourselves known to one another.

They told me straight out that my wife had died, calling her that, my wife rather than their stepmother. This was due, I am sure, solely to the fact that I had not recognized them at first when they had come in to me and thus I might not have known to whom they were referring if they had said only that their stepmother had died. I asked them if she had died without great pain, and they answered that she had died with eagerness, and I expressed my relief at that, for she had lived with great pain for many years, and they said that their knowledge of her life confirmed this observation.

The older of the two was the spokesman, it seemed, for his younger brother remained mostly silent throughout our interview, except now and again to interject a word or two for emphasis or clarification, such as, when the older brother had told me that the physician attending my wife had pronounced her dead of a congenitally distressed heart exacerbated by the depredations of poverty and a life of stress, the younger added the information that this was also how my first wife had died. That was how he referred to her, as my first wife, rather than as his mother, again doubtless because I had not recognized them when they had first appeared to me and thus I might not know who he was talking about if he had said, My mother.

Here a slight misunderstanding between us arose, for we were as yet unused to each other's company and our respective ways of expressing ourselves. I wished to know if my wife had died in her coffin, which of course is one of the rites which would have characterized her life and would have lent it meaning, if it had been followed properly, and which thereby would have provided us, her survivors in life, with the greater occasion to praise her, thus lending to our lives also a quantity of meaning they otherwise would lack. This circle is crucial to the maintenance of faith, as are all the rites, for no practice can evolve successfully into the sacred function of rite if it cannot stand the test of circularity. My sons, still boys, of course, probably had not yet arrived at the kind of informed worship of the dead (the faith that sustains itself by knowing itself) that would have let them know immediately my purpose in asking so quickly after being informed of her death if my wife had died in her coffin, because the older of the boys upbraided me with considerable feeling for my lack of feeling, as he saw it, and his brother grew stern.

But I was able to calm and smooth over their bristled words and glowerings against me by elaborating on the texts of several scriptural passages which prescribe the meaningful use of coffins during our life times, such as *The Book of Discipline*, xxxii, 12: Let the coffin serve up wisdom to the foolish, let it be a buckler for the timorous. For wise is the man who lies down in his coffin early in the day of his life time, and victorious is he who arms himself thereby. Also, xxiii, 4-5: This doth the dead hate, that a man come unto them naked and pretending like a babe that he was surprised by death.

My sons seemed pleased and enlarged by my explication and also by the rigor of my application of the said texts to the particularities of the death of my wife, their stepmother, so that in a short while we were all three quite at ease and hearty together in our praise of the dead, for they had admired their stepmother, my wife, quite as much as I, and it took no puffing up of our imaginations and language for us to tender mercy unto her. I was greatly relieved, needless to say, that my sons were able to give such abundant evidence of my wife's intellectual capacity and her dauntless energy for teaching them the basic articles of our faith, despite their lack of adult comprehension, for in the modern world where children are so cleverly and constantly cajoled into seeking transient pleasures and relations, it is not an easy or simple thing to drive them to the path of righteousness and meaning, and having got them there, to keep them from wandering off that path and getting all lost among the living.

ERE I shall enter into a description of certain afflictions which have characterized my recent months and have sorely tested me in divers ways. Know, however, that it has not been my belief in the worth of worshipping the dead and the eternal benefits that accrue thereby that has been tested, but my old decision, described early in this relation, not to resist life. I refer to my atonement for having failed my first jailor, John Bethel, so that he went unto death in my stead and bore with him my own coffin. He had not fully comprehended my teachings, even though he had become converted by me to my faith in certain of its aspects, and for that he had willed himself to sacrifice himself for the living, not yet realizing that the only worthwhile and meaningful sacrifice of one's life is for the dead. (*II Carol.* iv, 34-35.) In atonement for the cursoriness of my instruction and the stupidity of my plan to alter the court calendar, thus incriminating another in my crime, I had made over to my jailor my own coffin, and as he wished, he was executed while in it, praise the dead. But that was not yet sufficient atonement, I felt, and so I determined to sacrifice myself also. But because of the nature of my offense, and my desire not to make my sacrifice a way of life, which would have been reprehensible to the dead, for my penance thus would have been eternal, as was John

Bethel's sacrifice of himself, I chose instead to limit my penance by a certain measure of time, the which was the natural extension of my life time. Therefore, I moved henceforward to avoid all such activities and practices that could lead me into a fatal encounter with death. It meant that I should not deny myself any sustenance, any food, rest or medication or other physical comfort that in whatsoever way contributed to the further resistence of death. To be sure, I would not chase obsequiously after these substances like some life-clinging wretch, but I could not permit myself to deny them when they were necessary or when they were imposed on me.

For many years this penance was easily made. Prison food and prison medication, required only rarely, were more than adequate, and my cell and few furnishings therein provided me with adequate comfort, and on the few occasions when my life was threatened by the violence of certain prisoners, my cowardice, though it shamed me, also made it so that I was making my penance, for it kept me from foolhardiness and forms of reckless behavior. Too, I was rarely ill during the early years of my imprisonment, partly because of my constitution and partly because of the generally benign physical conditions of the prison. Also, until her death, I was tenderly looked after by my wife, despite her own failing health, so that whenever I showed any slight sign of illness, no matter how insignificant, she would hurry to me with medications and kindness and would quickly cure me.

After her death, however, and following hard upon the visit from my sons, there commenced my period of illness. It introduced itself to me modestly enough, so that, unawares, I did not protect myself against it, because, as yet a man of time is inevitably inclined, I saw each new affliction as separate and independent from the other and saw not at all any sequence or heaping up, and surely I did not suspect that I was entering upon a whole and lengthy period of illness. Therefore, when there came into the corners of my mouth and upon the bridge of my nose a small number of boils and hard chancres, I was not alarmed or even especially discomfited by them, and so I merely waited for them to leave as they had come, silently and in the night and without apparent cause.

They did not leave, however, although individual boils and chancres did sometimes soften so that the pus beneath could break through and drain from the sore, which sore, when it had fled, would seem to reappear in another part of my mouth or nose. During this time I also contracted the disease called favus, which is characterized by small yellowish crusts on the scalp with raised edges and depressed centers. The crusts have a peculiar odor, like that of a mouse nest, and the hairs in the encrusted areas become brittle, loosen, break and fall out, so that when the inflammation has passed, there are left blotches of baldness across the scalp. This condition did not seem to me a disease at the time, for while I had the disease I was aware only of the itching, which was irregular, and I did not discover the bald patches until sometime later. The peculiar odor, because it was indeed so like unto that of a mouse nest, I simply attributed to the presence in my cell somewhere of a mouse nest. Furthermore, I was also then suffering for the first time from a condition known as dry seborrhea, which affects the foreskin of the penis and is characterized by itching caused by an accumulation of a cheesy material consisting of body oils mixed with dead cells and other tissue debris, and thus I was somewhat distracted from the favus infection on my scalp.

The reader should keep in mind that I did not at this time know what was yet to come, and therefore each new affliction I regarded as the last in a series. When I had developed boils, I did not know that favus would follow and that dry seborrhea would follow the favus. Nor did I know, when the dry seborrhea had cleared somewhat, that I would soon be afflicted by neuralgia, the chief symptom of which is extreme pain that comes on in paroxysms and severe twitching of the muscles of the affected part, in my case the cheeks of my face and the muscles surrounding my mouth. These symptoms took expression as a sudden grimace, practically an open-mouthed but silent laugh, despite the pain, and thus I was often thought to be enjoying some private hilarity, when in fact I was not. To further confuse people, one of the boils from my mouth had relocated in my right ear, to be followed by another in my left, and soon the swelling in the canals had become sufficiently extensive to cause a temporary but total deafness, so that I could not know what was being said to me and thus could not answer questions with regard to the incongruity between my facial expression and the absence of anything particularly humorous in my immediate situation or surroundings.

Along about this time I began to reason that there was a connection between my various afflictions, however tenuous, and I grew fearful, yet none of my diseases were such that they could be cured by any treatment other than rest and cleanliness, which were my habits to encourage anyhow. Unavoidably, one affliction seemed to lead to another, so that one night during my sleep, the neuralgic twitching of the muscles surrounding my mouth caused me to bite into the meat of my tongue accidentally, which in a short time became inflamed, swelling the tongue exceedingly and leading to an ulcerated and very tender condition and also several abcesses there. This condition brought on a constant and copious flow of saliva and also made it difficult and very painful to speak. In a few days I observed that my gums as well had become infected, for they had grown spongy and tender and had puffed out and sometimes bled and from time to time oozed pus from between my teeth. And still there was little I could do to cure myself, except to provide myself with rest and cleanliness.

Here I became sufficiently ill that the jailor at last brought a physician unto me, for there had appeared on the skin of my chest several large thickly encrusted areas of a purplish color. These masses of granulated tissue and tiny abcesses, bathed in a thin film of pus, had come from within my lungs, the physician thought, and indicated a condition he named blastomycosis, which he speculated had been caused by some type of yeast infection somewhere in my body. When I had told him of my dry seborrhea, he chuckled and said that it surely explained the cause but gave not a hint for the cure, for there was no cure, except to treat the affected areas of the skin with certain chemical solutions, which he dispensed to me and which I assiduously applied, bringing about a small measure of relief. I was left, however, with a painful cough and more or less difficulty with breathing, and with chills and sweats in alternation, and an indisputably foul-smelling sputum, these all coming as a result of the lung infection, which the physician told me might in time abate of its own volition.

I lay in my cot for most of my days now as well as the nights and no longer moved outside my cell. The pain from my lungs and from the boils and divers other sores as had appeared across my body and from the neuralgia and the diseases that filled my mouth and stopped up my ears, and the continuous itching in the various parts of my body, made me shrink inside myself like some dumb animal cowering in a corner, and I began to fear that I might be compelled, by my commitment to my life time's period of penance, to live this way for a long time, and this brought me to conclude that my will to atone was being tested by the dead. I believed that the dead were trying me because there had come into my spirit during these weeks a longing to join them that was exceedingly strong and that was not altogether spiritual. Against this longing I brought forth numerous scriptures and remembered teachings from my youth and all my powers of reason, for this was now a clash that rang out continuously in my mind with all the noisesome fury of a great clash between armies. I know that I often wept and groaned aloud and thrashed helplessly through the long nights.

It was now that the physician began to attend to me daily, as if he did not expect me to live, and it was in that way that I learned of how the abcess in my lungs, when it had somewhat subsided, had created a certain amount of scar tissue adhering to the walls of the entry to my stomach, causing these walls to pull away and form a sac, which he called a diverticulum and which unavoidably, as the sac increased in size, filled with slivers of food. And when the particles of food decomposed there, the sac expanded still further until it had grown to the size of a tobacco pouch and had caused a foul odor and much pain and vomiting. As a joke, the physician told me that the best cure was starvation, for no matter how little I ate or what I ate, there was bound to be some small particle that would be drawn into this ever enlarging pouch. For several days thereafter I did indeed wrestle with the temptation to cure myself by starvation, but after a while I was able to overcome this test also and thus agreed to follow the physician's instructions and attempted to keep food from entering the sac by laying myself in such a position as to place the sac at a level higher than the entry to my stomach, with the mouth of the sac pointed downward, which is to say, by lying on my right side with my head and shoulders on the floor and my hips and legs on the cot. Thus I was able to take a small amount of nourishment, mainly in the form of dry crumbly cereals so that the few grains which, despite these precautions, nevertheless got into the sac, could be drawn out daily by the physician with his rubber tube and pump.

But the cure for one affliction is frequently the cause of another, and because my diet was now restricted wholly to sips of water and bits of dry cereal, I soon developed the symptoms that accompany the absence of acid in the stomach, abdominal pain, headache, ringing in the ears, and constant drowsiness, a condition which additionally led quickly to pernicious anemia, which brought with it extreme weakness, breathlessness and heart palpitations. My skin all over my body, such of it as was not inflamed with boils and various sores, was a lemonish color, and my feet and hands had puffed out grotesquely. It now seemed to me that I would surely succumb to the temptation to die, for to live meant only to contract yet another, more nearly fatal disease whose cure seemed to be a still worse disease. When I slept, which was only in brief spasms, I had furious dreams, and though I wished for those among the dead to appear to me there and to advise me and I often cried out the name of my wife or of John Bethel or of my parents, none from the dead came to me then. Only the living appeared to me, in my sleep as much as when I was awake, my physician, my jailor, occasionally a curious prisoner who might have heard my groans, until I was no longer able to tell when I was not sleeping from when I was not awake, for in both states did these people appear to me in wildly threatening postures with their faces horribly distorted, as if they themselves had contracted all my diseases and had grown as grotesque to look upon as had I myself.

Now there came upon my body a great fever, which lasted for about ten days and nights and brought with it profuse night sweats and continuous headache, and when it had abated, left me weaker even than before, with certain of my other afflictions somewhat worsened, such as the neuralgic pains in my face and the coughing and the various symptoms of the pernicious anemia. The physician who had taken a sort of scientific interest in my case, for it presented him with many ongoing puzzles, could not at first diagnose this fever, until there had followed several more episodes of about ten days each, coming as if in waves, each one leaving me afterwards weaker than before. These waves, he said, were characteristic of undulant fever, an uncommon disease among the population as a whole but not uncommon among those who are known to deal with the dead, for it is contracted and spread chiefly by having come into contact with a similarly infected body or carcass, but because the germ often lies dormant for years, it is very difficult to trace the path of contagion. Thus, since my calling long ago had been as a coffin-maker, the physician had swiftly concluded that I doubtless at some time long before my imprisonment had dealt with an infected corpse, and it was only now, in my weakened condition, that the disease had made itself known to me. There was no cure for the disease that the physician knew of, but the symptoms could be treated as they appeared, and because he was interested in the course of the disease and in containing its spread, he determined to stay close to me and treat me as kindly as he could. He thought that he might thereby learn something about the disease so as to be able to devise preventive measures against its future occurrence, especially among the prison population.

From my own perspective, that of the sufferer rather than that of the detached observer and attendant, the wave-like ebbs and flows of the fever created in my life a paradoxical series of troughs of easefulness, for when my body temperature rose, the numerous pains I had been experiencing throughout my body would seem to diminish, so that the higher the fever went and the longer it lasted, by that much was I released from the pain of my boils and other skin afflictions and the neuralgia and the lung abcess and the pain of hunger caused by the diverticulum and the several other related agonies of that time, so that I came to welcome the approach of each new wave, each new undulation, of the fever. Though afterwards I was left each time as weak as a newborn babe, I was able for a few hours to experience considerable clarity of mind, and despite the inflammation of my tongue and my infected gums and teeth, I was able to speak with a remarkable clarity.

During the attacks of fever, however, I was not aware of anyone who happened to be in my presence, nor was I aware of the passage of time, so that I had to be shown with a calendar how long each wave had lasted and told, with notes from the physician, for I could not understand his speech due to my deafness, who had attended me and what had been done for my comfort, information I desired so as to be able, during my periods of lucidity following the wave, to show my gratitude. In this way I learned of the physician's sustained efforts to cool my body by applying alcohol soaked sponges and the regular baths he provided for the removal of the stools and urine that I emitted while feverish and unable to care for such functions myself. I also learned that my jailor, too, and even his superior officers had taken an interest in my condition and had posted an assistant jailor to keep watch over me, so that at no time was I without someone keeping vigil.

During the first few onslaughts of fever, I felt as if I were in a dream, although I knew I was not sleeping, and there came to me numerous faces from among the dead, and they would speak soothingly to me, as if to strengthen me in my resolve not to resist life so as to keep my penance. In this way I was encouraged by my father and my uncle, and also my first wife and on another occasion my second wife, both of whom knew from their own lives how difficult and painful it often is not to resist living. There also came to me Justice Hale, who had died during the second year of my imprisonment and who now appreciated the wisdom of a faith that in his life time he had merely been willing to tolerate (which raised him above his brother judges, however, for none there were among them, except Justice Hale, who had been willing even to tolerate dissenters), and he too encouraged me in my resolve to exchange my life for John Bethel's death, for he reminded me of the foolishness of my desire in the beginning of my imprisonment to bring my case to a legal point.

Then there followed several more waves of fever, and no longer were the dead presenting themselves to me. In their stead came the faces of the living. First there came my second jailor Jacob Moon, who was wearing now a handsome pin-striped business suit instead of his old gray uniform, and he too tried to comfort me, but his words were of a different order than had been those of the dead, for he kept telling me that I should not fall into despair, for soon I would no longer be among the living. And my wife's cousin Gina, in the company of my five children, all of whom looked upon me with great sympathy and said that I had suffered enough and should give myself over from this penance. Mingled with these were the faces of my present jailor, and sometimes his assistants, and even sometimes that of my physician, and they were all saying to me the same thing, that I should let myself die now, for my sufferings had gone on long enough for many normal life times. There even came to me one of my own brethren in the faith, my friend of long ago who had counseled me to leave off the making of coffins and turn my skills to the manufacture of glass-fronted cabinets, and he once again gave me his sympathetic counsel, because of his love for me, and again it was counsel that denied my understanding of my own love of the dead, for he urged me to leave off my determination not to resist life.

Until there came at last the waves of fever in which there appeared to me the faces of both the living and the dead, and I could not tell one from the other, the living from the dead, although I knew them all, and they all counseled me and cajoled me and showed me great sympathy, and I loved them all for it and was grateful to them, even to those among them who said nothing, some living and some dead, who merely with their presence showed a concern for me, the Justices Bester and Twisdom of long ago, and certain of my brethren, and the infant born dead to my second wife, and many of my fellow prisoners, the party boys and the athletes and the philosophers, and even the knife boys and madmen who had wanted to do so much violence. Some among these were dead, and some were yet living, and the dead among them urged me not to come among them, to hold fast to my penance, and the living among them urged me to depart from them now, to join the eternal dead. And their voices were like a chorus that harmonized their differences and sent up a song of such precise beauty that I wept uncontrollably, for I loved them all so very much.

THOUGH my imprisonment continues, my relation of it cannot. I must bring it to a close. I have composed it during the interludes between the attacks of the undulant fever. My strength for this composition, despite the effects of my illnesses, has been given to me by my coffin, which was presented to me at last by the prison authorities when it seemed to them that I would soon die of a disease that could be spread chiefly by handling an infected corpse. For this reason, they came into my cell during one of my attacks, when I was not aware of their presence, and placed my body into a simple but adequate wood coffin, so that when the wave of fever had passed over me and I knew again where I was, I found myself lying in my coffin. My joy was great at this, and to the astonishment of my physician and the jailor, I was immediately given sufficient strength to use the periods of lucidity that followed each new attack of fever for the purpose of composing this relation. I asked for pen and paper that very day, and also a board to prop against the sides of my coffin, and as I lay there, I began to write. In no other way during my life time have I been able to tender this much mercy to the dead, as I do now, with this relation of my imprisonment, for it has been composed expressly for the use of the living, to whom I must now say Farewell.

This book was set in Garth type at
The Writer's Center, Bethesda, Maryland.

Typesetting: Barbara Shaw
Design Consultant: Kevin Osborn